Serenity

5/1/03

For Chuck,
Friend, mentor,
editor — And Joyce,
his lovely lady. You're
a wonderful couple.
So glad I know you!

Love,
Dixie

Serenity

Dixie Land

Alabaster Books
Kernersville, North Carolina
USA

Serenity is a work of fiction. Any references to real people, events, establishments, organizations, or locales are intended only to give the fiction a sense of reality and authenticity. Other names, characters, places, and incidents portrayed herein are either the product of the author's imagination or are used fictionally.

Published by Alabaster Books
P.O. Box 401
Kernersville, North Carolina 27285

Book design by Jeff Pate
Cover art by Janice Polanski-Beihoff of Franklin, Wisconsin

FIRST EDITION

Library of Congress Control Number: 2003091005

ISBN: 0-9725031-0-2

ACKLOWLEDGEMENTS

THANKS! To my best friend, number one enthusiastic supporter and constant sounding board, Larry. I couldn't have finished any of my novels without you. I love you.

My gratitude to my children Brad and Diane, for encouraging me from the start. A very special thanks! Alex, Ross and Ryan, you're a constant inspiration to me.

Linda, I'm so glad you moved here. I don't have to mail you my manuscripts any more.I appreciate all of you who have read my work, and liked it. You motivate me to continue my writing.

Chuck Smithers, what can I say? Thank you is far too inadequate for all of the time you gave to each of my manuscripts. What a favor you did me when you introduced me to Jan Beihoff. Such an artist!

My wonderful friends and writers of the Triad Writers Roundtable: Lynette Hampton, Chuck Smithers, Kathy Fisher, Joanne Clarey, Patti Morgan, Elizabeth Hedgecock, Dave Shaffer and John Staples; your input is invaluable. Chris Roerden; thanks for taking the time to answer my many questions in such depth. Jeff Pate, thanks for your willingness to help whenever I called. I am blessed that you've shared your artistic creativity with me.

Knowing each of you enhances my life!

For Jane and Ken,
Wish you were still here. I love you.
Thanks for absolutely everything.

Chapter One

Maggie Thornton squinted as the summer morning sun emerged from behind a cloud casting a blinding glare on the windshield of her green Ford Taurus station wagon. She adjusted the visor then slid her brown-framed sunglasses from the top of her head down over the bridge of her nose. She lowered her right hand and let it rest on the side of her neck. She was surprised to feel a little chill shoot across her shoulders and down her back as her fingers touched the tender nodules there. She began to knead them. Another testament as to how tense she had been without even realizing it.

An involuntary shudder shook her as the impact of her life-altering decision finally began to sink in. The tragedies of the past months had made this the most difficult year of her life. But this last situation, this discovery about Michael, had pushed her beyond her endurance. It had broken her; given her reason, or perhaps an excuse, to do something quite out of character for Maggie. She had fled everything: career, relationship, so-called friends and even location. She had retreated from it all. She must try to begin again.

She had completed her packing in the wee hours this morning, loaded up her car and left the furnished townhouse she had rented in Alexandria, Virginia, for the past year. She glanced at the clock on the dash and realized she'd been on the road for more than five hours. No wonder she was tense. She'd always hated long drives alone.

During the first two hours of the drive she had vacillated between tears and angry diatribes directed at Michael. She'd made a brief stop at a rest area to rinse her face and try to compose herself and hadn't stopped driving since.

"I need another break," she said aloud. " I'll stop at the next exit and stretch my legs."

As she continued on, she began to have doubts as to the wisdom of the decision that placed her on this North Carolina highway heading she wasn't quite sure where.

She had been close to tears when she handed in her resignation Friday at the end of her shift at Lee General Hospital. Her only measure of comfort in the entire day had come from what she perceived as genuine regret that Martin Forsythe expressed at losing her.

"You're one of my best staff nurses, Maggie, I don't want to lose you," the administrator had told her. "This is so sudden. What can I do to keep you?"

Maggie had pled personal reasons.

"Has something happened that I should know about? Do you want to talk about it?"

Her answer had been no.

"Then let's make it a leave of absence," Martin had said. "I know how difficult this past year has been for you. Maybe you just need a little time away."

She had consented and then felt guilty for the lie. But it seemed the most expedient way to end the discussion. She had no intention of returning to this hospital or even to the area ever again. After leaving the hospital administrator's office she'd gone directly to the hospital employee's credit union and had withdrawn her life savings of $4,500.37. She took $3,500.00 of it in traveler's checks and kept the rest in cash. Then she'd gone home to pack up her belongings. She'd worked into the night and all day Saturday to get her things together, clean the apartment, pay a few bills and write the necessary letters to utility companies and to her landlord. She hadn't slept before leaving, but she wasn't tired. All she wanted was to get on the road and away from everything that reminded her of Dr. Michael Kerns. He hadn't attempted to contact her, and for this she was thankful. He was the very last person on earth she wanted to talk to then and now.

She drove on several miles before she saw a road sign. *Serenity, North Carolina: 1 mile.*

"That sounds inviting," she said aloud. She always talked to herself when she drove alone. Maggie flipped on her turn signal and moved into the right lane of traffic.

When she reached the exit, she drove up a long curving incline and stopped at the stop sign. She made a right turn then drove down a slight incline into the most tranquil, quaint little village Maggie had ever been in. She immediately felt a sense of having been transported into the past. For the first time in months she felt a slight sense of comfort. All of the shops that lined the cobblestone-street looked as if they had been there for a hundred years, yet all of their exteriors looked freshly painted. The carved wood signs in front of the shops were hung from black wrought iron posts; neatly laid brick sidewalks formed a path between them.

Maggie drove past a bookstore, an antique shop, a library, a curio shop, drugstore and a pantry before coming to a row of frame houses. Daisies, phlox, lilies, hollyhocks and canna grew among the stately oak trees that lined both sides of the street. Their leafy heads linked in the center of the broad road forming an arch of softly filtered sunlight over the little community.

"Serenity is the perfect name for this lovely little spot," Maggie whispered.

Chimes broke the silence. In the distance she saw a church steeple. She drove on and stopped in front of the white-frame chapel. The sign in the yard read, "Welcome all. Leave your cares on the steps of the Lord's house. Sunday service, 11:00 A.M."

Oh gosh, it is Sunday! Maggie thought, and aloud she asked, "Why not?"

She glanced at the Timex on her arm; it showed 10:58. Not surprising there was no longer anyone going inside. She hoped her watch wasn't slow.

She found a parking place on a side street and stepped out of her car. She stood for a moment as she smoothed her denim skirt and red cotton pullover. She took a deep breath, filling her lungs with the delicate scent of jasmine and honeysuckle. A sudden breeze tousled Maggie's short wispy chestnut-brown curls and blew her skirt against her thighs as she hurried the short distance to the steps of the church. When she reached the top, she saw a large empty basket. There was a sign on it that read, "Care Basket, leave your excess baggage here."

"You don't have enough room for all the baggage I'm hauling," she said under her breath.

Maggie pulled open one of the heavy wooden doors. She stepped into the sanctuary as the preacher rose from his chair behind the pulpit and stood before the congregation.

"Good morning," he greeted his parishioners.

"Good morning," reverberated back.

Maggie slipped into the pew at the back of the church and sat down as the rest of the congregation rose, hymnals in hand, and began singing, "How Great Thou Art." She rose quickly as the little woman beside her smiled and moved her hymnal closer to share with Maggie.

When the song ended and the congregation was seated once again, the minister began walking down the center aisle toward Maggie.

"I'm happy to see we have a visitor today. Would you mind standing and telling us who you are, and how we came to have the pleasure of your company?" He stopped beside Maggie and offered her his hand. He was a tall slender man with wavy silver hair and gray-blue eyes. His voice was very deep but there was gentleness in his tone. As Maggie looked into his eyes, she was reminded a little of her late grandfather, Joseph Thornton.

Feeling flustered, she rose and put her hand in his as she cleared her throat. Maggie heard the rustling of people turning in their seats. She took a deep breath then began softly.

"I'm Maggie Thornton, and I'm a registered Nurse. I'm in the process of relocating, and I stopped in Serenity to take a driving break. Your town and church looked so charming and inviting to me that I wanted to join you for the service."

"I'm Reverend Donald Townlee, and we're all so very glad you're here, Maggie Thornton. Welcome."

The parishioners punctuated the minister's welcome with applause.

"Today is our homecoming," Reverend Townlee continued. "We'd love to have you join us after the service for a delicious meal. I can guarantee you won't go away hungry. And, wait till you taste Martha Walker's apple pie." He rolled his eyes, and a wide grin transformed his face to that of an impish little boy. Turning around to where Martha was seated, he asked, "You did bring the pies didn't you, Martha?"

The woman beamed at him as she nodded.

"Thank you. You make it sound tempting," Maggie said. "I'll give it some thought."

The minister released her hand and returned to the pulpit. The woman next to Maggie leaned toward her, touched her arm gently and whispered, "Might as well stay. We have some mighty good cooks around here, and you have to eat someplace."

An hour later the service ended with the singing of "Just A Closer Walk with Thee," and the parishioners, perhaps one-hundred people, filed out and began to mingle outside the chapel. The woman Maggie had been sitting beside walked out with her.

"I'm Lillian Bingham, but everyone in town calls me Lil," she told Maggie. " I work at the drugstore just down the street. You had to pass it when you came into town." Lil's ready smile was so broad that her blue eyes crinkled until they nearly shut as she looked up at Maggie.

"It's good to meet you, Mrs. Bingham," Maggie said smiling back at her. "You've made me feel very welcome." She studied the little woman's round face peering up at her from beneath a bright pink straw hat, complete with plastic strawberries and daisies attached to the brim. It appeared to have come straight out of the nineteen forties. Maggie couldn't help but wonder just how many churches she'd have to visit before finding another bonnet quite like this one that adorned Mrs. Bingham's graying-locks. This quaint little town with its friendly people truly seemed a world apart from the hustle and bustle of Alexandria.

"Now, Maggie honey," the woman continued, "you call me Lil, and you'll make me feel comfortable. And, tell me where you're headed."

"As I said—I'm going south."

"Where south, Honey?" Lil pressed.

"I… I haven't made up my mind which city," Maggie confessed. "But somewhere in Georgia." She was relieved to have Reverend Townlee join them. Perhaps Lil would stop asking her questions.

"So, Maggie Thornton, have you thought over our invitation and smelled that appetizing aroma long enough to decide to join us?" As he spoke, he guided the women toward the side yard of the church where several ladies were arranging large bowls and trays on tables that had been set up beneath green and white striped canopies.

"I think I really should head on, but thanks for the offer."

"Nonsense!" Lil chimed in. "She doesn't even know where she's going."

"Is that right, Maggie Thornton?"

Maggie didn't reply.

"You'll have to excuse Lil. When she thinks somethin' she doesn't keep it to herself. She's got a good heart, and everyone knows that's where it comes from. We love her." He said putting his arm around Lil's shoulder and smiling down at her. "Why Lil, I think you're blushing."

The apparent affection between the two was comforting to Maggie.

"That's alright," She said with a chuckle. "No offense taken." She found herself liking this chatty little woman in her pink print cotton dress and straw hat. And she liked this kindly old preacher who called her by her full name each time he addressed her. She felt more comfortable here in this beautiful little village, with these folksy people, than she had felt anywhere else in a long time.

"Do you have family, child?" Lil asked.

"Actually, I don't. I… that is to say… I have two aunts—one in Savannah and one in Macon, Georgia. They're the only family I have left and that's why I'm heading south." She didn't add that her aunts had no idea about her plans, and that she hadn't even checked to see if they were at home before she packed up and left Virginia.

They both looked at Maggie in silence. She continued.

"My father and my only sister were killed in a plane crash over Wyoming about a year ago. You may have seen it on the news." She could feel that old pain creeping into her chest. "My mother died of cancer a couple of months ago," she concluded softly. Suddenly she was acutely aware of someone's eyes on her.

She shifted her gaze to her right. It was the same woman who had turned to look at her several times during the church service. Now that woman approached her. A tall man with graying hair followed a few steps behind the woman.

"Mornin' Caroline, Charlie," Lil said with a nod.

"Mornin' Lil," the woman replied without taking her eyes from Maggie. She stopped in front of Maggie. The man waited several paces behind her.

"Maggie," the newcomer said softly.

There was something so compelling in her sad, gray eyes as she looked at Maggie that Maggie couldn't take her eyes from the woman's. She felt as if they were making a spiritual connection. For that instant, Maggie felt as if they were the only two people standing in this beautiful churchyard.

"Maggie," the woman began once more. "I want you to stay with Charlie and me."

Lil and Reverend Townlee drew in a breath in unison.

Caroline didn't seem to notice. "We have a furnished apartment over our garage, and I want you to stay in it if you need a place to live. You can stay for as long as you want."

Maggie was at a loss for words. She didn't know these people, yet they were offering her the sanctuary she needed, and she felt strangely comfortable with them. It seemed eerie to her. Actually, from the moment she had entered this curious little village, the entire morning had seemed a bit surreal to her.

"That's all right, child," Caroline said tenderly. "No need to give me your answer now. Stay and eat dinner with us, and we'll talk about this later." She embraced Maggie ever so briefly then turned and walked to her husband. He wrapped his arm around her, and they headed toward the food tents.

Maggie watched the couple for a moment before turning back to Reverend Townlee and Lil.

"Maggie," Lil said so softly that it was almost a whisper. "Do you have any idea what just happened?"

Chapter Two

Maggie shook her head. "No. Other than that a very nice lady with sad looking eyes offered me a place to stay."

"I hope you'll consider her offer," Reverend Townlee said. "That is if you don't have any definite plans, Maggie Thornton."

A man across the churchyard caught the minister's eye and beckoned.

"It appears I'm needed. It's almost time to ask the blessing. You ladies come along now; don't let the food get cold." He hurried on ahead of them toward the tents.

"Maggie," Lil began wide-eyed, "what just happened with Caroline, that was wonderful! And I think I know what triggered it. I noticed her watching you during the service, and I could see what she saw. I knew just what she was thinkin', cause I thought it too."

"Thought what?"

"It's this, Maggie girl. You put her an awful lot in mind

of her daughter Joy."

"I do? I still don't understand, Lil."

"Joy was up at Carolina getting her nursing degree two years back, and she and her fiancée, Jason Porter, left to come home for the weekend one Friday night. It was late, after her three to eleven shift was over. A drunk driver ran a stop light and plowed into them. Both of 'em were pronounced dead at the scene. It was one of the saddest times I can remember in Serenity. Jason was in medical school, and they was both gonna come back when they graduated and open a clinic here, sort of take some of the load off of Doc Miller. He, by the way, is lookin' to hire another nurse."

"Oh, Lil, that's so sad." Maggie could certainly relate to the awful pain of losing those you love. She had lost five people she loved in the last year. "Losing loved ones tears at your very foundation," she said softly. She could feel her eyes moistening.

"Well, Maggie, until today Caroline's been shut up in her own grief, if you know what I mean. She hasn't reached out to anyone. Lord knows I tried to comfort her. We used to be quite close. Plenty of other folks have tried to help too, but it just seemed no one could get through that wall of sorrow she's pulled up around herself. But today—today she reached out to you. I hope you're gonna take her hand. It could do you both a world of good. I sense you're carryin' your own powerful load of grief."

"I'm not sure what the right thing is for me now." Maggie's eyes were still misty. "When I stopped here an hour-and-a-half ago it was to take a break from driving. Now, a short time later, I'm being asked to consider making Serenity my home. And, I find myself actually thinking about the possibility."

"You just keep considerin', honey. That's all we can ask." They reached the food tents. "We'd better get in line before this good food's all gone."

By the time she reached the desserts, Maggie's plate was close to overflowing. There was fried chicken, beef stew, barbecued ribs, ham, country ham, stuffed pork chops, squash casserole, broccoli in cheese sauce, green beans, corn, mashed potatoes, sweet potato casserole, potatoes au gratin, and the list went on. Even a smidgen of everything that looked good was impossible to fit onto a dinner plate.

Lil introduced Maggie to everyone in the double line, and they chatted as they loaded their plates. Maggie picked up napkins and flatware while Lil looked for a place for them to sit.

"Lil, over here."

Maggie looked in the direction of the rich baritone voice. A tall, well-built man with dark brown hair rose from his seat and gestured. Maggie thought him quite handsome except for the melancholy look in his eyes. This was the second person in Serenity with that same sad expression. Was there any connection?

"Ross." Lil waved back. "We'll be right over." She leaned toward Maggie's ear. "Come on, honey. You have to meet our town pharmacist. And there's Doc Miller and his wife, Kathryn, sittin' across from him. Did I mention that Doc's lookin to hire a nurse?"

Chapter Three

"Thanks for the help, Mr. Keller," Maggie said as the older man laid the last of her suitcases on the floor in the living room of the apartment over his and Caroline's garage. "I hope you haven't strained your back. Some of my boxes were pretty heavy."

"Whew!" Mr. Keller sat down on the couched and wiped his brow with his shirtsleeve. "A couple of them were right heavy. For the life of me I don't know how a little girl like you got 'em in your car all alone. And Maggie, I wish you'd call me Charlie like every body else does."

Maggie laughed. It had been a long time since anyone had referred to her as a little girl. It felt comforting to have this fatherly attention. "I'll try— Charlie," she said still smiling. "My parents were sticklers for Mr. and Mrs."

"I understand," Charlie said good-naturedly. "Oh, before I forget, Caroline wanted me to tell you she's expecting you for dinner around seven-thirty or so."

"That's very generous, but I'll just find a bite somewhere. I'm really tired, and I need to spend the evening unpacking. You two have done enough for me today."

"It's you who've done for us, Maggie. Caroline's so pleased that you decided to stay in the apartment. I can't tell you the difference in her since she met you today. When you get all settled and rested, I'll tell you a bit about what the last couple of years have been like for Caroline. We sure would love it if you'd decide to come eat with us tonight. We'll set a place for you, but if you don't make it I'll understand." Charlie rose and started toward the door.

"I'll try to come. And thanks again for everything."

He stepped out of the apartment and closed the door. Maggie heard his footsteps fade as he trudged down the steps.

She could feel the moisture welling in her eyes at this couple's kindness and concern. Then thoughts of Michael and why she had fled Alexandria, flooded through her mind, and the tears spilled onto her cheeks. How could she have been so wrong about him? He'd been so charming, seemed so eager to please her. Theirs had been such a whirlwind courtship. But he'd seemed so sincere, so genuine about his feelings for her. And she'd been so vulnerable. He had asked her to marry him after only a few weeks. She had put him off, but he'd been persistent and she'd finally accepted after six months. Then her mother became ill quite suddenly, and Maggie had insisted the wedding wait so she could devote all her spare time to caring for her terminally ill mother.

"Stop this! It's useless. And it's over!" She told herself as she dried her tears.

Maggie reached for the largest of her three navy-blue and tan suitcases. "Wow," she groaned, "this *is* heavy. How did I manage it alone?" She half carried; half shoved it into the cozy little bedroom and hoisted it up onto the bright pink blue-and-yellow patchwork quilt that adorned the double bed. She straightened herself to her full five-foot-seven inches and ran her hand down over her lower back. I must be tired, she thought, and then she tried to remember when she had slept last. "No one should go that many hours without sleep!" she scolded. She opened the suitcase and began unpacking as she reflected over the last hours.

She shook her head slowly as she worked. She was still having trouble believing that this morning she had been headed for Georgia, either Macon or Savannah, she wasn't certain which, and this evening she had decided to stay in Serenity, North Carolina, at least for a little while. She liked everyone she'd met today. They were all so friendly, just plain folks as they referred to themselves. It was so refreshing after the revelations she'd had in the last few days about two of the people she had trusted most.

Lillian Bingham was very much the mother hen looking out for her throughout the afternoon. She had the distinct feeling that Lil had a little matchmaking in mind between Maggie and Ross Harrington. But that was the last thing Maggie was interested in now or any time for that matter. She had a very bad taste in her mouth when it came to tall, dark-haired, handsome men. Anyway, she had learned that he was divorced, so there must be something wrong with him. She planned to keep her distance. Still, she couldn't help liking Lil. The friendly little woman had made her feel at ease, protected, from the moment Maggie sat down next to her in the pew.

And Caroline and Charlie; they had joined Lil, Maggie and the rest of the folks at their table for dessert. Caroline had watched Maggie and smiled at most everything she said. Then Caroline had gradually joined in the conversation.

Maggie hoped she was doing the right thing by agreeing to stay here, that it would be right for Caroline as well as for herself.

Two hours later the white French-provincial dresser drawers were filled, her clothes were hung and shoes were neatly arranged on the floor of the small walk-in closet. She hurriedly made up the double bed with the fresh linens Caroline had sent up with Charlie. She glanced at the watch on her arm and was surprised to see that it was seven-thirty.

She decided she would have dinner with Caroline and Charlie, but she'd make it an early evening. Tomorrow she really should call Aunt Clara and Aunt Emily to let them know where she was. Though they didn't see one another very often anymore, her aunts did call her occasionally, and if they did and found that her phone was disconnected, she knew the elderly ladies would worry. And, she didn't know how she was going to explain her reason for leaving Alexandria. For the time being, it was all too fresh and hurt too much to discuss with anyone.

She started out of the room and caught sight of her reflection in dresser mirror. She tucked her blouse in and straightened her skirt. She gave her hair a quick once over with her brush and pinched her cheeks for color, then headed for the door.

She walked down the stairs and stepped out the door into the back yard. As the heat hit her, she felt a slight wave of nausea, or maybe it wasn't the heat so much as the humidity coupled with fatigue and hunger. Charlie was on the far side of the yard picking some tomatoes and cucumbers from their garden.

"Charlie," she called waving at him. "Sorry I'm late. The time just got away from me."

"Don't think nothin of it, little girl. I got used to it living in a house with two women all those years." His voice trailed off.

Maggie was silent. She looked around the yard; someone had put a lot of time and work into it, and it was lovely. There were tomato plants, cucumbers, green beans, squash, and butter beans. Behind the vegetable garden was an American-beauty red rose garden bordered by white impatiens. Maggie walked over and bent down to smell one of the roses.

"My absolute favorites," she said. "Did you do all this,

Charlie? Your garden looks like a page out of *Southern Living*."

"I do everything but the roses; they're Caroline's babies. They were always Joy's favorite too." He smiled at Maggie. He seemed pleased that she appreciated their efforts. "For a while it was Caroline's only link to sanity during some of those early dark days. She said it connected her to Joy."

"I'll love looking out of my windows with a view like this." Maggie noticed the basket he was filling was just about to overflow. "Here," she said reaching for the cucumbers he was trying to balance on the top, "let me carry those." With hands full, she started for the back door.

"Go right on in, little girl. Caroline's expecting you."

As she reached the house, she stopped at the foot of the stone steps to admire the border flowers. Here more impatiens grew, a mix of red and white, with delicate white baby's breath laced throughout them. It made the immaculate white frame home with its shiny black latticework shutters look like a big dollhouse.

Maggie turned back toward Charlie and, seeing that he was busy with his vegetables once again, she gathered her skirt up in front of her to make a deep pocket and dropped the cucumbers in so that she could rap lightly on the door.

"Come right on in, dear." Caroline was busy at the stove and whatever she was cooking smelled delicious.

When she turned to smile at Maggie, the first thing Maggie noticed was Caroline's blue-gingham bib apron. Maggie's grandmother had always worn one when Maggie was little, a bib apron and a smile. It was one of her fondest memories of Granny Ellen. Whenever Maggie saw her, with her white curls cut short about her face and her wire rimmed spectacles sitting on the bridge of her nose, bustling about the kitchen, she thought Granny Ellen would have been the perfect model for a Norman Rockwell painting. Though Caroline was a bit younger, she would also fit the bill for a Rockwell creation.

"Dinner smells wonderful! I can't imagine how I could

possibly feel hungry after the way I ate at the homecoming, but the smells in your kitchen make my mouth water, Caroline."

"I just put boneless chicken breasts into some pasta with a can of soup, a little butter, cheese, mushrooms and garlic. Then I sprinkled on a few crushed seasoned croutons to top it off. Nothin' fancy, but it does smell good, doesn't it?" Caroline's soft voice had a melodic quality to it. "I'm glad you came, Maggie."

Their eyes met and held for a moment. Maggie thought Caroline's had brightened a bit from earlier this afternoon.

Charlie clomped into the kitchen and plunked his basket of vegetables on the counter.

"Whew!" he let out a deep breath and mopped his brow with his shirtsleeve again then quickly glanced at Carolina as if she might disapprove. When she didn't seem to notice, he continued. "That humidity's about to do me in."

"Why don't you get washed up for dinner, Charlie," Caroline told him. "I'll cut up some tomatoes and cucumbers for now, and we'll get the rest of this washed and put away later."

Maggie took the flatware that Caroline handed her into the dining room and arranged it on the cream-colored lace tablecloth that covered the antique cherry dining room table. Then she helped Caroline carry the food in to the server. When they were seated, Charlie asked the blessing. At the end of his prayer, he thanked God for leading Maggie to Serenity. She found it quite touching.

Maggie wasn't disappointed; dinner was as tasty as it smelled. She surprised herself and took seconds. The iced tea was marvelous, better than any she could remember. It had a bit of a spicy taste, and there was definitely a hint of mint in it too. Maggie drank two glasses. When they finished eating, Maggie yawned. "I'm so tired, I really need to go back to my room and get some sleep."

"I stuck a peach cobbler in the oven just before we sat

down. It was Joy's favorite. It'll be done in less than twenty minutes," Caroline said, "Why don't you rest on the front room couch until it's ready. I'll fix you a bowl to take with you; then you can leave."

"I'll wait for the cobbler, but let me help you with these dishes," Maggie protested.

"Nonsense," Caroline said softly. "You can hardly hold your eyes open. Charlie'll help me. He's used to it."

Maggie went into the living room and sank down onto the overstuffed floral slipcovered sofa. It felt wonderful! She took a deep breath and closed her eyes, not to sleep, but just to rest them. She could hear the sound of a mixer, or something humming in the distance and muffled voices as she allowed herself to drift off.

More voices...but she couldn't understand them. They seemed to be speaking in a strange tongue. It wasn't Spanish or French or anything Maggie had ever heard before. Someone approached her. It was Caroline, and Charlie was beside her. They were looking down at her, and suddenly they began to laugh and point at her. When they opened their mouths their teeth were jagged. As they leaned over her, Caroline's eyes took on an eerie red glow. Maggie tried to get up but she couldn't seem to move her legs. She looked at Charlie. He was holding something with both hands. It was the pitcher of iced tea. As he glared at her his skin began to sag and hang down from his face and neck.

"It was the tea," he said mockingly in a gravelly voice. "It was that good, good tea."

Maggie screamed, and suddenly she was aware that her legs were moving and her arms were flailing about but reaching nothing. She opened her eyes and Caroline was leaning over her calling her name softly.

"Maggie, Maggie. Child, what is it? Charlie and I were out in the kitchen when you let out this blood-curdling scream. You must have been dreaming, Maggie, and it must have been an awful one. Are you alright now?"

Maggie sat up and looked around. Charlie was at Caroline's side.

"I think Maggie's over-tired," he said. "I think we need to let her go back to the apartment and get a good night's rest."

"Charlie's right. I'll dish up some cobbler for you now. And we'll check on you in the morning. Charlie asked Milt from the Phone and Communication Company to come by tomorrow morning and get service hooked up for you."

Caroline walked with Maggie to the back door and gave her hand a little squeeze as she left. The woman stood in the doorway as Maggie crossed the lawn to the garage.

Midway across the yard Maggie stopped and turned back. "Thanks again."

"Good night, Joy," Caroline called melodically as Maggie reached the door to the stairs.

First that horrid dream and now this! A cold chill ran all the way down Maggie's spine.

Chapter Four

Despite her fatigue, it had taken Maggie quite some time to settle herself enough to fall asleep. She had decided that she would pack up first thing in the morning. She couldn't stay on here. The nightmare had been unsettling, but Caroline calling her "Joy" in that tone of voice had been the clincher. It really had jangled her nerves, so badly in fact, that she had pushed one of the living room easy chairs against her door after locking it.

Maggie stirred from her night's sleep to the sound of footsteps on the stairs. She bolted up in bed and squinted from the glare of the sun shining through the east window of her bedroom. Someone pounded on the door.

"Who's there?" she called out in a firm voice. There was another knock followed by silence.

"Who's there?" she spoke louder.

"It's Milt Ainsley, from down at the phone company. Charlie asked me to come by and hook up your service. Sorry if I woke you."

"I'll be right there," she said, hopping out of bed and grabbing her robe as she started for the door. She opened the door a crack, "Sorry for your trouble, but I've decided I won't be staying after all, so I won't need a phone."

"Outside wiring's all done so all I need to do is connect it inside. You might as well let me bring it on in, and they can cancel it as soon as you're gone."

"Okay," she said reluctantly. She did need to call Aunt Clara in Augusta and let her know she was on her way. She'd leave some money for the call on the dresser when she left.

Milt let out a heavy sigh and asked, "Are you gonna let me in now, or do I need to come back later?"

"Just a minute," Maggie said. She closed the door and pushed the chair out of the way then opened the door for Milt. He stepped inside.

"Wonder where the best place to put this is?" he mumbled to himself.

He noticed a phone jack at the far end of the living room and started toward it.

"Sure is too bad about Caroline, ain't it?"

"What are you referring to?" Maggie asked.

"She had a relapse late last night. Mrs. Eller across the street said she saw Doc Miller's car pull up about eleven-thirty last night, and he didn't leave 'til nearly one this morning."

"Really?" was all Maggie could muster. She began to feel very uncomfortable again.

"Poor Caroline. She," he corrected himself, "they've been through hell. They tried for years to have a child; never could. They finally adopted Joy, and she was their life, Caroline's and Charlie's. When she died, it was like Caroline died too. She'd been doing a bit better lately, and then yesterday at the homecoming she seemed like a new woman. Everyone noticed it, and we thought when you decided to stay it seemed like a tonic for her. You look a bit like Joy, ya' know. Same coloring, height. Yeah, as a matter of fact, you favor her a lot."

Maggie shivered; she felt the hair on her arms bristle.

Milt turned to look at Maggie, "That'll do it, your phone's connected now."

"Thanks, Mr. Ainsley." She wanted him to hurry and leave so she could get on with her packing.

"Folks are sure gonna be disappointed that you're leaving, Maggie." He was at the door now. "Just tell Charlie to let me know when you're gone, and we'll turn off the service."

"Thanks. I will." She heard his footsteps fade as he descended the stairs.

Maggie felt sad for Caroline, but she was no psychiatrist. She wasn't the person who could help her. She had her own problems to deal with. She hurried into the bathroom and splashed cold water on her face. Then she went out to the kitchen and opened the refrigerator door. It was empty except for the peach cobbler she had placed there last night. She removed it and sat down at the kitchen table. She took a bite. It tasted delicious. After two bites such a strong wave of nausea washed through her that she barely made it into the bathroom in time.

When she felt it was safe to leave the bathroom, she went into the living room and dialed Aunt Clara's number. She let the phone ring fifteen times. There was no answer. She looked up Aunt Emily's phone number in her address book; she never could remember the Savannah area code. She dialed her Aunt's number. The phone rang six times. "Oh please, please pick up, Aunt Emily," she whispered.

As if her aunt had heard her plea, she heard, "Hello."

"Oh, Aunt Em. It's Maggie. I'm so glad you're home." Maggie's voice broke.

"What is it, my dear? What's wrong?"

'I want to visit and maybe stay for a while, Aunt Em. Is it all right?"

"Oh my, yes, Maggie! How exciting! You're always welcome here. You know that. Aunt Clara's visiting. And wonderful news! Your Michael's on his way here, too. He called looking for you last evening, said you'd disappeared, and he thought you and he needed to talk. Oh my, I'm so glad you called, dear, because his call really worried Clara and me. Not letting people know where you are, that's not like you."

"Oh no, Aunt Em. I don't want to see him, and he and I don't have anything to discuss."

"Nonsense, Maggie. He must be a good man. He's a doctor. I thought you two were in love, that you were to be married. You should always be willing to talk your differences over, dear."

"No. There's nothing to say," Maggie said stubbornly.

"Oh my, Maggie. It's too late…because he thought you'd show up here, and he's on his way as we speak. He's flying in at one o'clock and renting a car. He'll be here at the house by mid-afternoon."

"Then I can't come. I'll call you in a few days. I love you, Aunt Em. Aunt Clara too."

"Wait, Maggie, where are…?"

Maggie put the receiver down and made another dash for the bathroom.

Chapter Five

Maggie filled her smallest suitcase first then sat down on the bed for a moment. Why was she so nauseated today? She put her hand to her forehead.

Her skin felt normal to the touch, and she didn't feel feverish internally. Was there something wrong with the food? No. She was being paranoid now. She thought of Caroline, and a melancholy feeling swept through her. She decided to take a break from her packing, dress and go down to tell Charlie and Caroline she was leaving. Then she'd come back and finish. She was going to need Charlie to help her carry the heavier pieces, especially the way she was feeling this morning. She certainly didn't relish the thought of getting on the highway, and she had no idea where she was going now that Michael was headed for her refuge.

She dressed, went downstairs, took a deep breath, knocked on the back door. She stood trying to decide how to begin. Within a few seconds, Charlie opened the door slightly and seeing Maggie his face broke into a broad grin.

"Good mornin' little girl. Come on in," he said opening the door.

"I can't stay. I came to tell you that I'll be leaving later this morning. How is Caroline? Mr. Ainsley from the Phone Company told me she had a bad night."

Charlie's face fell. "She did have a bit of a bad time after you left."

Doc Miller came over and gave her an injection to help her calm down and get some rest. She's still asleep. Maggie, I'm so sorry about last night. I heard what she said to you when you left; I heard her call you Joy. And I hate that you feel you have to leave." Suddenly, Charlie looked spent.

"I'm sorry too, Charlie, but I don't think my being here is helping Caroline. I know you've both been through a heartbreaking experience. Believe me, I know what it's like to lose those you love. But I'm afraid my being here will only aggravate her situation."

"I hear what you're sayin', Maggie. You know though, for most of the day yesterday I felt like I was getting my old Caroline back. She smiled and talked and cooked again."

"Charlie," it was Caroline's voice. "Do I hear Maggie out there with you?"

"Yes, darlin'. I'll be there in a minute."

"You better go on, Maggie. I'll tell Caroline when you leave. Let me know when you're ready, and I'll come carry those suitcases for you."

Before Maggie could step out the back door, Caroline entered the kitchen. "Maggie," she said quietly, "I'm afraid I made you uncomfortable last night. I'm sorry, dear, I know you aren't Joy. And I know Joy died in that awful accident and that nothing is going to bring her back." She wiped a tear from her cheek. "I don't know what happened to me last night. That was the fullest day I've had in a long time. Maybe I was overtired just as you were. I hope we can put it behind us and go on from here."

Charlie's eyes widened in amazement. He stepped toward her and kissed her forehead. "Caroline, I'm glad you..." he paused and nodded toward Maggie as if to say, I'll handle telling her if you want to go back and finish packing.

"We will put it behind us, Caroline," Maggie felt a little awkward. She wanted to put Caroline's mind at ease, but she also wanted Charlie to be the one to tell Caroline that she was leaving. From observing Charlie's protective nature with Caroline, Maggie knew that he would find the right words.

As she walked toward the garage, Maggie said a little silent prayer that Caroline would take the news without regressing. She seemed in such a delicate state.

Halfway up the stairs Maggie felt so dizzy that she had to sit down on the step. Her skin became clammy, and the nausea returned. "Maybe I have the flu," she told herself. After a few minutes the feeling eased. She finished the climb, went into the apartment and headed for the bedroom. She put the largest of her suitcases on the bed and began to fill it. She reached onto the closet floor for a dress that had fallen off its hanger and her hand bumped her box of tampons. Then it hit her; her period was late! And she had always been so regular.

"Oh, dear God," she implored, "don't let it be that. Please don't let me be pregnant. Not on top of everything else in my life right now!" They had been careful; Michael had used protection.

She put her hands on her breasts; they felt tender. She stepped in front of the dresser mirror, unbuttoned her blouse and looked at her nipples. "Oh, no, no, no!" She sobbed. "This can't be happening to me."

Chapter Six

Maggie called Doc Miller's office mid-morning on Monday to say she wouldn't be in. Then she spent the rest of the day in bed. On Sunday afternoon she had accepted a position at the clinic. She was supposed to have an orientation this afternoon. She hoped she could make it on Tuesday.

Last night she had decided to stop by on her way out of town and tell the Millers she had changed her mind and wouldn't be staying in Serenity. But she couldn't travel feeling like this. It appeared she'd need that job for a time anyway. Necessity had forced her to make the only decision that seemed feasible for now.

Caroline looked in on her several times during the day. She brought Maggie chicken broth, applesauce and ginger ale and acted quite normal. She seemed to enjoy having someone to take care of.

Maggie couldn't bring herself to confide to anyone just yet as to what the real cause for her illness was. She knew she was going to have to see a doctor soon, but whom? Perhaps when she was feeling better she would just go some place completely new and make a fresh start. She could say she had been widowed and.... There were just so many things to consider. The more she thought, the more her head began to throb, and the more nauseated she felt.

By evening she had managed to keep down a bowl of chicken broth, a cracker, two tablespoons of applesauce and two small glasses of ginger ale as well as some water. Her head had stopped pounding, and she felt somewhat human again.

About seven thirty her phone rang. For a moment she considered not answering, but on the fourth ring she picked up the receiver.

"Hi, Maggie, It's Lil. I got your number from Milt. I called over to Doc's office this afternoon to see how your first day on the job was going. They said you had some sort of stomach virus. How are you feeling now, Honey?"

"How nice of you to check on me. I'm doing much better this evening," Maggie told her.

"Shall I come by, Maggie? Is there anything you need?"

"Thanks, Lil, but Caroline's been up several times today. She's taking good care of me. I don't need anything, but you're very thoughtful. I appreciate your call."

"I'll phone over to Doc's tomorrow and see if you made it in, Maggie. Take care." Maggie heard the click as Lil hung up. She smiled. Lil was quite the busy little character.

...

When Maggie awakened Tuesday morning she felt refreshed and, all things considered, quite good. She didn't want to chance getting on the road quite yet, so she decided to go in to work. She could tell Doc at the end of the day that she wouldn't be staying long. She'd leave it up to him if he wanted to hire her under those conditions.

By mid-morning Maggie was still feeling good, and she

found herself genuinely enjoying assisting this small town doctor as he went about his busy schedule. Many of the patients they had seen this morning were people Maggie had met at the homecoming. Just before lunch they heard scuffing, loud voices, and screaming mixed with crying coming from the waiting room. Doc was finishing up with a patient. He left the examining room and went out into the waiting area.

"There, there now, what's all this cater-walling about?" he asked in a firm but kindly voice. "Bobby, son, that's enough now," he told the small blond boy with big brown eyes who was creating the ruckus.

The boy's left hand was wrapped with a bloody terrycloth hand towel. On seeing Doc, Bobby quieted down for a moment.

"Now," Doc said, "Come with me, Bobby, and let me have a look at that hand of yours."

Bobby allowed Doc to guide him toward one of the examining rooms. Doc motioned to Maggie to join him then turned back to the harried mother and said, "We'll call you if we need you to come in, Sarah."

His mother looked relieved as she took an empty seat in the waiting room. Doc took Bobby into room number two and lifted him onto the examining table. Maggie followed. She reached for a suture kit and opened it. She picked up a bottle of Lidocaine and a syringe. When Bobby saw the needle and realized what Maggie was preparing was for him, he began to scream again.

"Bobby," Doc said quietly, "I want you to tell Maggie about spiders, I hear you're quite an expert."

Bobby stopped crying and looked at Doc. "Who told you that?"

"I heard you talking to Jerry Weston yesterday at the picnic. From what I heard, you're very knowledgeable."

Bobby grinned at Doc then at Maggie. "I am," he said. "Go ahead. Ask me anything." He concentrated his full attention on Maggie.

"Well… I have so many questions I hardly know where to start."

Encouraged, Bobby completely ignored Doc as he unwrapped the bloody wash cloth, injected the Lidocaine and set to work suturing Bobby's index finger. Bobby began with the definition of arachnid and went from there.

Maggie was quite impressed. This five-year-old sounded like an encyclopedia on spiders when he got started. When he wound down about ten minutes later Maggie said, "Believe me, Bobby, if I ever meet any folks with questions about spiders, you'll be the one I send them to."

"That's it, Bobby. We're all through," Doc said, sliding him gently off of the table.

Bobby looked at his left hand in complete surprise, then he grinned. "I was brave wasn't I, Maggie?"

"Yes. You were, Bobby. One of the bravest boys I've seen in a long time— smart and brave. That's an impressive combination." Maggie started toward the door with Bobby. He reached for her hand and held on tightly until he was back in the waiting room with his mother.

"I sure was brave, Mom," he boasted.

"That he was," Maggie said. "He was a real little soldier. Not one tear the whole time Doc was suturing him up."

His mother looked surprised and even more so at what happened next. She and Bobby had started toward the door when Bobby broke away from her and ran back to Maggie. He threw his arms around her waist and whispered loudly, "I love you, Maggie. I'll be back to see you."

Kathryn Miller, Doc's wife, had been observing from the reception area. "You should consider that a real compliment, Maggie. He doesn't warm up to many people like he did to you. His parents don't have a lot of patience with him, and he can really be a handful at times. Guess we know who'll be in charge of Bobby's appointments from now on."

Midway through the afternoon, Doc asked Maggie to call the drugstore to see if they'd received their shipment of Bactroban. Lil answered.

"Maggie, good to hear your voice," she said. "I tried you at the apartment and figured you must be at work when there was no answer. Hold on, honey, and I'll check for you." A couple minutes later, Lil returned to the phone. "We got a whole case of it this morning, so tell Doc he can prescribe to his heart's content."

"Thanks, Lil."

"Wait a minute, Maggie. I want you to come have dinner with me tonight." Maggie had planned on a quiet evening by herself, to try to make some decisions about her future but she heard herself ask, "What time?" And say, "I'll need some directions."

They decided on seven-thirty. It turned out that Lil lived just a few blocks from Maggie's apartment.

The last patient left the doctor's office at six o'clock. Maggie was tired, but all in all it had been a very pleasant day. She liked Doc and Kathryn Miller and the receptionist Mildred. Maggie learned part way through the day that she was Kathryn's widowed sister. She was very helpful and welcoming of another nurse to help carry the workload, as she had had to work the examining rooms as well as the desk when things got hectic. Yes, Maggie had certainly had worse first days than this on a new job.

Maggie arrived back at the apartment at five after six. Five minutes to get home from work certainly did beat the forty-five minute drive through heavy traffic she'd been used to in Virginia. This morning she had planned to begin some packing when she finished at the clinic. By the end of the day she had failed to mention to Doc how temporary she considered this job. She decided to postpone leaving. She would stay here in Serenity a short while longer. She'd get to feeling better and save some money. She was definitely going to need more money now.

...

Maggie took a quick shower then slipped a mint green sundress over her head. She stepped into the closet and slid her feet into matching green sandals. She tried to pull her chestnut locks into a ponytail, but her hair was still a little too short to stay up. She brushed her hair back from her face and dabbed on a little lipstick and Mascara. She went into the living room to watch the news. Peter Jennings appeared on the screen as she heard a knock at her door.

I'll bet it's Caroline, she thought. "I'm coming," she called. She reached the door and opened it.

He was tall, lean and handsome with his dark brown hair tousled just a bit. Maggie's breath caught in her throat.

"Michael!" she blurted out.

A kaleidoscope of emotions flooded through her at the sight of him: anger, hurt, betrayal, hate, and yes, she had to admit it, love. The heart doesn't suddenly stop loving the man who has been such an important part of your life simply because the mind commands it, no matter how he's deceived you.

Chapter Seven

"Maggie, we have to talk." His green eyes looked so appealing.

Maggie managed to find her voice. "How did you find me? I didn't tell my aunt where I was." Her stomach churned; she felt close to tears.

"Your aunt has caller I.D. I made a couple of calls, rented a car, and here I am."

"Michael, after what you've done, I don't think we have anything to talk about. Nothing on earth you could say could change what I saw in that hospital room." Her voice was shaky as she recalled the scene she had stepped into.

"I know, I know. There is no explanation." He hesitated, "And no excuse for it. You're the girl I love, Maggie. I'd give anything to change it."

She could feel her cheeks burning, she knew they must be crimson. "You have a rotten way of showing your love, Michael."

"Maggie, I know it was wrong but I'd been so overworked and stressed out, and you'd been so pre-occupied with your mother and..."

"Oh, my God, Michael! Pre-occupied with my mother?" Maggie began to sob. "My mother was fighting a losing battle for her life. She was dying, and you knew it. You're a doctor for God's sake. Have you become that callous that you can only think of the cost to you? Where were you when you weren't working? You should have been there at my side. After what I saw in that hospital room, I can only assume you were off somewhere rolling in the hay with my so-called best friend the other times too. Not only did you wound my soul; Robyn crushed it too. And now..."

"Maggie, I'm sorry," he interrupted. "Like I said, I'd change everything if I could. I do love you, but…"

"Change what, Michael? Getting caught?"

He paused a moment and put his hands on her shoulders and leaned his head down toward her as if he were going to kiss her. She pushed his hands away and stepped back.

"Please, don't touch me, Michael," she said firmly, though inside she felt herself beginning to waver. His mellow voice and that little boy look he got on his face when he was trying to talk her into something always grabbed at her heart.

"Okay, Maggie. Okay. Sorry. I won't touch you," he said backing away and raising both hands into the air. "I have to tell you something. And you aren't making it easy on me. I wanted to do it in person; I wanted you to hear it from me not someone else. I've got to do the right thing. Robyn's pregnant, and I'm going to marry her," he blurted out. "I'm sorry, Maggie, so sorry. Because I still love you."

His words struck her like a dagger of ice thrust into her chest. Her breath caught in her throat, she felt weak, chilled to her very core. She was silent as she fought to maintain her composure.

She took a deep breath before replying to his bombshell. "You've said what you came to say," her voice was strained. "Now I want you to leave."

"Robyn wants to talk to you." Now Michael sounded unsteady. "But—she doesn't know what to say." He paused. "She feels awful too."

"It isn't necessary. There isn't anything she *can* say. Just leave, Michael. Now!"

He looked at her for a moment as if he wanted to say something else. Then he shrugged, turned, walked to the door and exited without another word. She heard his footsteps on the stairs. Then the door slammed shut, an engine revved, then silence.

She stood transfixed, tears flooding down her cheeks. After a moment she walked over and sank onto the couch. Sobs shook her body. "Oh, Michael, how could you do this? I loved you. I trusted you," she whispered. "How could I have been so wrong about you?"

Even though she'd been the one to leave, to end the relationship, perhaps there had been just the slightest hope in the recesses of her mind that something would happen; some nebulous fairy-tale explanation would be given to reverse it all. Now, this made it forever final. It hurt terribly, even though she knew this was the only way it could be.

It really didn't matter whether Robyn was pregnant or not. Maggie knew she could never be with a man she couldn't trust. If he had cheated once the odds were he'd be tempted again, and it would probably be easier to succumb the next time. This was right; there was no other way. At that moment, she vowed that she would do whatever it took to keep him from finding out about *her* baby. From this day on, she'd think of this child as hers and hers alone. There was absolutely no place for Michael in their lives.

...

She sat for some time swept up in her grief before remembering she had promised Lil that she'd have dinner with her. She couldn't go now; she wouldn't be fit company for the devil himself. She looked for Lil's phone number in her purse and couldn't find it. She couldn't remember Lil's last name to look it up in the phone book. She'd just go to the door and tell Lil she couldn't stay, that she wasn't feeling well. That was not a lie.

She went into the bathroom and splashed cold water on her face and re-touched her makeup. She went downstairs and got into her car.

Charlie was in the garden again and when he saw her he waved and called out, "I see your young man found you, Maggie. Didn't stay long, did he? Oh well, enjoy your dinner with Lil. She's a real fine cook."

She nodded at him and started the engine. Did everyone in town know her business? Maggie pulled out into the road and made a left at the corner. Lil lived a few blocks down the street on the left in a light gray cottage with black shutters.

Maggie parked her car in front of the house and walked up to the door. She barely got her hand on the knocker when Lil opened the door.

"Maggie, I'm so glad you made it." Lil gave her a little squeeze. "Come on in, honey," she said pulling Maggie into the living room and closing the door. "And look who stopped by. I always say, the more the merrier."

"Hello, Maggie." It was Ross Harrington's mellow baritone voice.

Ross looked surprised to see her there. Evidently Lil had meant the dinner as a little surprise for both of them. A bit of the match making that Maggie suspected Lil had in mind at the homecoming. The last thing on earth she was interested in tonight or any other night. She didn't think she'd trust any man ever again.

"Have a seat, Maggie," Lil said, motioning toward the opposite end of the sofa on which Ross was seated.

Maggie looked around and sat down in a green overstuffed glider rocker. "Lil, I can't stay. I, I'm not feeling well. I didn't have your phone number, so I just came to say that I couldn't come," she said awkwardly. She rose from the chair.

"Now Maggie, you need some food in you, and I've made a big skillet of hamburger pie. Stay and help me get rid of it. Then you can go."

"Me too, Lil. I need to get back to the drugstore and shelve the rest of the shipment that was delivered late today."

"I can do that first thing in the mornin'," Lil offered.

"Thanks, but I've been waiting for that Verapamil. They've assured me that it's in this shipment, and I need it for Jake Hansen. If it's there, I want to drop it by his house tonight on my way home."

"That's good of you, Ross. You're right; I understand," Lil conceded. She excused herself and went into the kitchen.

There was an awkward silence. Maggie's mind spun from one topic to another, but she could think of nothing to say to this man.

He broke the silence. "This is kind of embarrassing, isn't it?" he said smiling at Maggie. "Subtlety has never been one of Lil's strong points. What do you say we just chalk it up to her good heart and enjoy our dinner?"

Maggie smiled for the first time since she had opened the door to Michael. "That sounds good to me. It's a deal."

Conversation ceased to be a problem. The two found they had a lot in common, and it seemed no time at all until Lil returned to say dinner was on the kitchen table. It was a "good ol' home cooked meat and potatoes dinner" as Lil had promised, and it was delicious.

When Lil got up to clear the table, Ross excused himself. He turned to Maggie; "I enjoyed talking with you. Maybe we can do it again sometime." He touched Lil's shoulder as he passed her, "Thanks, Lil. See you tomorrow."

After he left, Maggie said, "Let me help you with these dishes, then I should be going too."

"You might be sorry, honey. I don't have a dishwasher."

Maggie stacked the dirty dishes, carried them to the sink and picked up a dishtowel. "My grandmother didn't have a dishwasher either. I loved helping her with the dishes. That's when we had some of our best talks." Maggie's mood had improved considerably once her initial discomfort had been overcome. She had even managed to push her anger for Michael to the back of her mind for the present.

Lil ran a sink full of hot water. She squeezed in a generous amount of Dove and swished it around with her hands. She turned to Maggie. "Girl, I hope you weren't upset with me for invitin' Ross over too."

"Well I have to admit it threw me a little. Ross seems like a nice guy, but I'm not looking to meet *anyone*."

"It's not what you think, Maggie. I just thought you two could be friends. You have a lot in common; your background in medicine and all. And, you've both had your hearts broken." Lil looked Maggie in the eye. "I'm right, ain't I? I can tell it in your eyes."

"Is it that obvious?"

"Maybe not to everyone, but it is to me cause it happened to me, too." Lil shook her head. "Guess for as long as I live I'll carry it with me." Lil was quiet for a minute.

"Where do these dinner plates go?" Maggie asked.

"Just stack 'em on the table, honey, then I'll put 'em all up together when we're done." She continued her scrubbing in the sink. "As I was sayin', Maggie, I've been there too. I was married to Henry Bingham for fourteen years. The last two were pure Hell." Lil's voice was suddenly filled with emotion. She stopped her washing, and wiped her hands on her apron. She took a Kleenex from her skirt pocket and dabbed at her eyes before blowing her nose.

Maggie was silent, allowing Lil to take the lead. If Lil wanted to tell her more she would, Maggie thought. She didn't want to ask questions that would upset her new friend any more than she already was.

"Look at me blubberin' all over myself," Lil said, trying to smile. "Every time I let myself think about that situation I end up like this."

"Maybe you need to let it out, Lil," Maggie heard herself say. Maybe she should take her own advice, but this wasn't the time or the place for it.

"I guess you're right, and I have let it out. Lots of times. Maybe one of these times I'll be able to let it go. Everyone tells me I need to, and I know they're right. But knowin' and doin' are two quite different things."

Maggie smiled at her and nodded, "You're so right about that."

"Stay a while longer. I'll put on a pot of green tea. It's good for lots of things." Lil busied herself putting the clean dishes into the cupboard, then removed a box of tea from the top shelf and put two bags into the carafe of the automatic coffee maker. She filled it with filtered water. She motioned Maggie to sit at the kitchen table. "This'll be ready in less than five minutes."

"I really didn't intend to stay so late," Maggie said as she obediently walked over to the chair she had occupied during dinner and sat down. She guessed Lil needed company tonight, and it had been good for her too.

When all the water had run through, Lil poured them each a mug of the steaming tea and brought it to the table. She took the chair across from Maggie.

"I'm gonna let it out one more time, Maggie, and then I'm really gonna try to bury it." Lil took a deep breath. "Like I said before, the first twelve years Henry and I were married were pretty good. Oh, we had our little problems but nothin' we couldn't handle. Then his kid sister got cancer and died. She was a single mom; had a boy twelve and nobody to take him but Henry and me. Kevin, that was his name, had a real rough time copin' with his mother's passing. Henry didn't have much patience or understanding about it. I'm not sure why, but he didn't want to talk about it, and he always ended up yelling at Kevin.

"Henry had started drinking heavily, and couldn't nobody get through to him that it was only makin' matters worse. We fought about every day, and I know it was miserable for Kevin. He withdrew even more into himself. Then one day Kev didn't come down to breakfast. I went up to his room and knocked on the door. After a couple of times, with no answer, I went in. The bed was made and the closet was empty. He didn't leave a note or nothin'. He just disappeared, and there's never been a trace of him since. It's awful not knowin'." She sounded distant, as if she were far from her kitchen table and Maggie.

After a moment she resumed her story. "I could tell Henry blamed himself 'cause he promised he'd quit the drinking, but he just couldn't seem to go for more than a day before he'd be right back at it. I wanted him to join AA. He said he didn't need them, that he could do it on his own. But he couldn't; it had a hold on him." She shook her head. When she looked at Maggie again there were tears in her eyes.

"Then, one night in December, we'd had a terrible argument and I told him it was over. That I couldn't take any more and I was leavin'. He promised me again that he'd stop. I told him I couldn't believe him anymore. He grabbed his coat, and stormed out of the house. As he was leavin' he said, 'You'll see.' I didn't know what he meant.

"Danny Fortis, from the highway patrol, came to my door two hours later to tell me Henry 's car had hit an ice patch on a bridge and had gone over the side. It landed twelve feet below at the bottom of the ravine. Henry was dead. They found a piece of paper on the front seat with the address and phone number of Alcoholics Anonymous in Fayetteville scribbled in Henry's handwriting. I guess that's where he was goin' when he was killed. That's what he meant by, 'You'll see.'

I should've given him another chance."

She seemed to be talking to herself now. "If we hadn't quarreled, and he hadn't left so mad, he wouldn't have had that accident." As she ended, her voice sounded very matter of fact.

Maggie reached across the table and put her right hand over Lil's, but she remained silent.

"Thanks, Maggie. Thanks for what you didn't say, because I've heard it all from others before, and it doesn't help. I have to be the one to tell me and convince me of it. No one else can do it for me."

After a moment, Maggie pushed her chair back and stood. "It's getting late and my six o'clock alarm will be ringing all too soon, Lil. I really need to leave."

Lil rose too and walked with Maggie to the front door. "I wonder if Ross got that medicine to Jake," she said. "That Ross, he's such a good man. He deserved a whole lot better than he got. Why do the good seem to have the bum luck, Maggie?"

"I suspect it all evens out. We all get a share of the good and the bad. Though sometimes the bad does seem to come in bunches," Maggie said pensively.

"Ross sure seems to be havin' his bad." Lil didn't appear to want Maggie to leave before she brought the conversation back to Ross.

"His wife Melanie ran off with one of our pharmaceutical salesmen," Lil began. "It was goin' on practically under his nose, but he refused to believe it. I guess he just loved her so much that he couldn't see any of the bad in her that the rest of us saw.

"This town was too small and evidently too tame for Melanie. Her father had been career military, and they'd lived all over the world. She thought she wanted to settle down and stay in one place, but before a year was up she was restless as a grasshopper in a field of tobacco. She stuck around for another year, but she was meetin' that salesman behind Ross' back every chance she got. Everyone knew it but him. Doc finally talked to Ross and made him see what was goin' on. When Ross confronted her she didn't deny it. He was still willing to put the past behind them and give it another try, but she wasn't. He wanted a family, she didn't. And she didn't want to be stuck in Serenity for the rest of her life. Serenity was the last thing she was looking for. She wanted excitement!"

"I'm sorry for him. But it sounds like she did him a favor by leaving, if that was the way she really felt."

"She did." Lil agreed. "But, oh, she disappointed him, and what she did hurt him so deeply."

"It's terrible when someone you love betrays your trust like that." Maggie felt a little chill run through her stomach and chest as Michael's appealing green eyes appeared in her mind's eye. "Terrible," she repeated softly.

Maggie opened the door. "Thanks for a delicious dinner and good company, Lil. I'll talk to you soon."

Lil stood in the doorway until Maggie was safely in her car and had started the engine. "Good-night," she called as Maggie pulled out into the road.

As she drove the short distance back to her apartment, Maggie reflected over all she had learned this evening. In a few short hours she was getting quite an earful about Serenity's citizens. It was beginning to sound anything but what the name and first impressions of this beautiful innocent looking little community had implied!

Chapter Eight

Though she hadn't intended to stay long, one day then two had stretched into nearly three weeks. She had to admit to herself that she really had nowhere else to go. Where else would her secret be safe? Certainly not with either of her aunts. They were so eager for her to end up with Michael, *a doctor,* that she felt they'd do anything within their power to try to reunite them. She wouldn't trust them not to let news of the baby slip should he get in touch with them in the future, remote as that might be. She certainly didn't want to fill her two elderly naïve aunts in on the sordid details of Michael's betrayal. Besides, she liked her new job and the friends she was making in Serenity. It was much more comfortable for her to remain here for the present.

One thing she was certain of was that she was going to have to confide in Doc soon, because good prenatal care was essential. She had become very conscious of eating well and drinking plenty of milk even though she had never liked it. She was also careful not to skip meals, and that took some planning with the busy schedule of trying to keep up with Doc and the multitude of patients he managed to see daily.

Toughest to give up was the coffee. She could drink decaf, but it wasn't the same. Like so many other R.N.'s, it had been a staple in her diet since her early days in training. She had also started taking a multivitamin with iron every day. She wanted nothing but the best for this little one who had already been deprived of a loving father. Yes. She could put it off no longer. She would stay on at the end of the day and talk to Doc.

Kathryn and Doc usually did the cleaning up at the end of the day together. This afternoon, Maggie would offer to relieve the older woman of that chore.

"You're a true angel of mercy," Kathryn told Maggie with a chuckle when she made the offer at five-thirty that afternoon. "I have so much to do tonight that I didn't know how I was going to fit it all in. Thank you, my dear." With that, Kathryn grabbed her sweater and bustled out the door.

Maggie went from room to room straightening, refilling dispensers and checking the instrument drawers. She and Doc ended up in examining room four at the same time. When they had finished, Doc turned to Maggie.

"You're a good nurse, Maggie, and a very thoughtful young lady. Kathryn and I are both grateful for the day you stopped in Serenity. You've taken so much of the load off of her. She tires more easily than she used to. I appreciate your staying tonight so she could leave a little earlier than usual."

Maggie felt a twinge of guilt.

"For that matter, Maggie, you've been looking a bit tired by day's end too. Are you feeling alright?"

This was the perfect opening, and yet she couldn't find the words to begin.

"I'm..." she stammered, "I'm fine."

"Well then, I guess we're finished for tonight. I'll see you in the morning, young lady." He hesitated, waiting for her to leave the examining room. She started for the door but stopped before she reached it.

"Doc, there is something I have to talk to you about." She could feel the color rising in her face and neck. She turned to look at him. "I'm quite sure I'm pregnant," she said simply. She fought the tears that began welling in her eyes to no avail.

He stood silent for a moment then stepped forward. He opened his broad arms to her. She buried her head against his shoulder.

"That's all right, Maggie. Go on and let it out," he said softly. "It's Okay. I thought you had something on your mind that you needed to talk out."

"Oh, Doc," Maggie pulled back to look at him. "I feel so alone in this. I can't marry the father. I don't even want him to know about it." Her voice was unsteady.

He took a Kleenex out of the box on his desk and handed it to her. "Why are you trying to protect him from this? Is he married? Even if he is, he has a responsibility here."

"I'm not protecting *him*, Doc. It's a gut feeling I have. I'm protecting my baby and me. It's a long story. He's a doctor at the hospital where I worked before I came here. We were engaged and were planning our wedding. My Mother became very ill, and we had to postpone our plans. I spent a great deal of my off-duty time with her. Then one day I stepped into an empty hospital room to make sure it was ready for a new admission we were expecting, and there he was, on the bed with my best friend. I resigned at the end of my shift, went home and packed up my belongings. I ended up here in Serenity. He found out from my aunts where I was and came here to tell me that Robyn, the girl he was with, is pregnant. That he's going to marry her. I don't ever want him to know about my little one."

Doc nodded. "I can understand perfectly how you feel, Maggie. That's a powerful load for one little girl to carry. I'm glad you told me." He patted her shoulder. "Now—have you seen a doctor yet? Do you know how far along you are? You certainly don't look pregnant."

"No. And I'm not sure. I want you to take care of me if you will."

"Of course, I will, Maggie. Of course, I will. We can examine you now, if you want. Come on, let's go down to room three." He stepped into the hall, and Maggie followed him.

...

Doc had made the situation very comfortable for Maggie, and she was grateful. He had determined her to be about six to seven weeks along. Everything looked good. He had drawn blood, and it would be sent to the lab in Fayetteville the next morning.

Before she left, Doc took a bottle of Ultra Natal Care vitamins from his sample closet. "This will save you a little money and a few explanations for now," he told her as he handed it to her.

"Thanks." Maggie smiled at him. "You've been terrific. You've made a tough situation…"

"Here, here now. See you in the morning, Maggie." He gave her a wave and a wink as she left the office.

...

By Saturday, Maggie was more than ready for the weekend. She slept until nearly ten. The morning sickness had eased some since she had confided to Doc about her condition and had been reassured by the examination that everything was as it should be.

Doc told her he wasn't concerned about it, that he considered the morning sickness to be a helpful thing.

"It helps remove some of the toxins we get from food

and other sources from both mother and baby," he'd said. "I've believed that for a long time, and now it seems some smart scientist is doing research on it."

Though she still tired more easily than before, it was wonderful not to feel those waves of nausea as the day wore on. Whether or not it was harmful, it was certainly unpleasant to feel that way. She hoped once these new vitamins really got into her system, that the fatigue would lessen also.

She had several errands to run today, and she needed to do some grocery shopping. She missed the large supermarkets of the metropolitan area she had moved from. Serenity had several convenience stores but only one family owned grocery store. And, while their product line was good, they lacked the variety of the larger markets she was accustomed to.

She went into the kitchen and fixed herself a bowl of oatmeal and a piece of whole grain toast for breakfast then took a leisurely shower. She hastily scribbled a shopping list and gathered up a bundle of clothes to take to the cleaners. By the time she was ready to leave, it was afternoon. The grocery store and cleaner were in opposite directions, so she decided to go to Parson's Market first. That way, she could drop the groceries by her apartment, put up the perishables and finish up the rest of her business on the other end of town.

She ran into several of Doc's patients as she shopped. She visited briefly with each, and by the time she was ready to leave the market, forty minutes had flown by. She smiled to herself as she got into her car recalling the many times she'd shopped in Alexandria and had never seen a familiar face with the exception of the checkout clerk.

She spent forty-eight dollars and had four large bags of groceries. Prices were a tad higher here, but the produce, being local, appeared much fresher, and the service was wonderful. Mr. Parson himself had wheeled her cart out and put her bags in the car for her.

When Maggie pulled into the driveway of her apartment, Caroline was in her rose garden. "Afternoon," she called out as stood and wiped her brow.

"Hi, Caroline. You look industrious today."

Caroline leaned down and cut three crimson roses and brought them to Maggie. "Do you have a vase for these, Dear?"

"They're absolutely gorgeous! I have a crystal vase that will be perfect for them. It belonged to my mother," she added.

"Let me help you with these groceries," Caroline said picking up two of the bags. "If we do this together, we can have them all upstairs in one trip."

"Thanks," Maggie returned, grateful for the help.

After she put the sacks on the kitchen table, Caroline turned to leave.

"I was just sayin' to Charlie that we hadn't seen much of you this past week. We miss you, Maggie. Why don't you plan to have Sunday dinner with Charlie and me? We'd love it."

"You and Charlie have done too much for me," Maggie said, removing the crystal vase from the cupboard and filling it with tap water. "Why don't you let me cook dinner for you tomorrow. Parson's had their pot roasts on sale, and I'll cook that with some potatoes, onions and carrots. Maybe I'll even throw in some of those fresh string beans Charlie left at my door yesterday. What do you say?"

"That's real sweet of you, Maggie. Yes. If you really want to that sounds delightful. Let me fix a dessert and some homemade bread."

"Great. Let's plan to eat at six," Maggie said. She arranged the three roses in the vase, carried them into the living room and placed them on the coffee table.

Caroline paused at the door. "We'll see you tomorrow. You can ride to church with us and, thanks for the dinner invitation."

Maggie nodded at her. "See you in the morning. And, thank you."

Both she and Charlie had been so kind, inviting her to dinner, bringing her fresh vegetables. Caroline had even offered to do her laundry. Maggie wouldn't hear of it, but the offer had meant a lot to her. Maggie's being there really seemed to be good for Caroline, too. She seemed grounded these days, and she was becoming much more extroverted. Even some of Doc's patients had commented on the difference they had noticed in Caroline over the past several weeks.

She heard Caroline's footsteps descending the staircase as she put up her purchases. When she had everything stored away, she glanced at her watch.

"Where does the time go?" she asked aloud. She grabbed her handbag and hurried back down to her car. She waved at Caroline as she pulled out of the driveway and headed for the cleaners.

After dropping the clothes off she heard her stomach growl. She decided to get something to eat before going over to browse at the curio shop. She crossed the street and walked the short distance to the As You Like It sandwich shop, opened the door and stepped inside. She was surprised to find all of the tables full at this late hour. Everyone there must have decided to be as leisurely as she today.

The shop's owner, Carl Warner, greeted her. "It shouldn't be long, Maggie. The Morris', over there in the corner, are almost finished."

"Thanks Carl, not a problem. I'm not on any time schedule today."

She heard the door open and close behind her.

"Hi, Ross," Carl said. "See you made it early today."

"Yep. And I'm taking the rest of the afternoon off."

Maggie turned to face him. "Hello, Ross," she smiled up at him. "Good for you! I think your schedule is about as hectic as Doc's."

He laughed, and his smile lit up his whole face. Maggie found Ross quite good looking. Standing here beside him, she became aware of what a big man he was. Not only was he tall, perhaps 6'3" or 6'4", but his frame was large. His white lab jacket emphasized the broadness of his shoulders.

The couple at the corner table stood and headed for the cash register. Carl motioned to a young woman across the room to bus the table.

"It's gonna be a few minutes before I have another table, Ross," Carl told him, "Unless you and Maggie don't mind sharing. What do you say?"

"It's fine with me, if Maggie doesn't mind."

Maggie nodded. "I never did like eating alone."

Carl led the way to the table and handed each a menu. "I'll give you a few minutes, if you'd like."

"Thanks, Carl." They said in unison.

Maggie decided on a chicken-salad sandwich on wheat bread. She opted for fresh fruit over the French fries that were offered.

"And I think I'll drink milk with that," she added.

Ross ordered a double bacon cheeseburger with a large order of fries and iced tea.

"It's been a long time since I ate breakfast, and they cook a great burger here."

Carl had just left with their order when Maggie felt a light tap on her shoulder. "Hi, Nurse Maggie." It was a child's voice.

Maggie turned to see Bobby Hensley, the little boy who had cut his finger during her first day at the clinic. Bobby held his hand up.

"See?" He grinned broadly, exposing the gap where his two front teeth had been. "You made it all better."

"I can't take the credit, Bobby. It was Doc and your own body that made you all better." She took his outstretched hand and gave it a little pat.

He reached into his pocket then held his hand out to her. "This is for you." Maggie opened her hand, and he deposited a miniature Hershey crunch bar into it.

"Thank you, Bobby. How did you know they're my favorites?"

"I just knew. They're mine, too," he said, cocking his head to one side and grinning again.

Sarah Hensley reached their table, "I'm sorry for the intrusion, Maggie. Hello Ross." She nodded at him before returning her attention to Maggie. "I just mentioned that I saw you across the room, and Bobby jumped right out of his seat and headed for you."

"I'm glad you came over, Bobby. I'd have been disappointed if you hadn't. The finger looks great! You can come speak to me anytime."

"Okay," he said. He gave Maggie a quick hug. "Oh, bye, Ross," he added. He walked obediently beside his mother, looking back a time or two, until they reached their table.

"I'd say you've made a conquest." Ross grinned at her. "I seem to be second rate with you around. Bobby's a great kid, inquisitive and bright as they come. Because of it, he's a bit of a handful for Sarah and Matt. Matt's considerably older than she is. And, they got a late start. Sarah was forty-one when Bobby came along. He's full of energy, and I think he might be just a little smarter than they are."

"He is bright," Maggie agreed, "and a little cutie, too."

"I've had some interesting conversations with him down at the drugstore. He's curious about everything; retains an amazing amount of what you tell him, too."

Their lunch arrived. The chicken salad was the best Maggie could ever remember. The pickle that accompanied it was delicious too. When Maggie commented on it, Ross told her Carl's wife put them up. "It's one of the reasons folks come here," he said. "The other being that it's the only lunch place in town."

Maggie laughed. "Since it's the only one, we're sure lucky it's so good, aren't we?"

Carl brought them separate bills. Ross picked Maggie's up along with his. "No really," she protested, reaching to take it from him.

"I'd like to, Maggie. Let's just call it a belated welcome to Serenity Maggie Thornton lunch."

"Thanks, Ross."

They walked outside together and chatted for a few more minutes. Maggie had to shield her eyes from the sun as she looked up at Ross. She found herself studying his face. Looking at his features separately, they all had flaws, but, together, they fit quite handsomely. Short dark hair framed his broad square face with its slightly crooked Roman nose. Firm lips gave him a look of strength. But, what she found most prominent about Ross, were his sad eyes. They were blue; and when he looked at her, she felt their intensity and their pain.

Maggie knew, from what Lil had told her, that they held deep within them a wound that he had tried to bury. But she suspected he'd have to try long and hard to get beyond it, if he ever fully could. And she could certainly relate to what he'd been through. Her heart went out to him. They'd had a very pleasant lunch, they both needed a friend, and she felt comfortable with him. Yes, Maggie decided at that moment, she liked Ross. She felt they had embarked on the beginning of true friendship today.

There was a pause in their conversation.

"Good-bye, Ross. Thanks for the lunch and the company." She smiled at him.

For a moment he looked as if he were going to say something, but he remained silent. Maggie turned and started toward her car. When she reached the door and turned to look back, Ross was right behind her. She gave him a questioning look.

"Maggie." He said softly. "I've enjoyed spending time with you today. What would you say if I asked you to drive over to Fayetteville with me tonight and take in a movie?"

Maggie was thoughtful for a moment.

"Not a date. Just two friends going to a movie together."

His eyes did it for her. "Okay. It sounds like fun. Do you have any idea what's playing?"

He smiled at her. "No. But we can go down to the drugstore, look at a newspaper and find out."

Chapter Nine

In the ten days since Maggie and Ross had seen *You've Got Mail* in Fayetteville, they had fallen into the habit of talking almost every day, either on the phone or in person. The evening had been fun. They'd found a theater that played releases that had been out for a while and both had wanted to see the Tom Hanks-Meg Ryan film. They weren't disappointed. In the closing scene, the Tom Hanks character walks over the hill with his dog as Meg Ryan's character waits nervously to see who will arrive. Meg tells him she was hoping he'd be the one to come. At that point, Maggie fumbled in vain for a Kleenex to dry the tears that were spilling onto her cheeks. Without even looking at her, Ross had passed her a clean popcorn napkin. Then he'd sat there patiently watching the credits until Maggie composed herself. She thought it very sensitive of him. She hadn't realized that his eyes were a bit moist, too.

Neither had spoken until they were outside and headed for the car. "I've always been a softie for a good romantic movie," Maggie confessed. "I absolutely loved that one."

"It was a good one. But then, any movie with that pair is bound to be good."

They stopped for a shake at a Cook Out drive-through before heading back to Serenity.

The following Monday, Ross called the clinic office to speak to Doc. When they finished their conversation, he asked for Maggie.

"How are you today?" he asked casually. "And how did your dinner with Caroline and Charlie go?"

She had mentioned to him, on Saturday, that she was a bit nervous to be cooking a meal for Caroline whom she considered a superb cook.

"It turned out great, and between the three of us we ate every bit of it," she said chuckling. "It was a good cut of meat, and I let it cook a long time. Caroline told me that was the secret, and she was right."

"Good," he said, "I knew you'd do fine. I enjoyed our movie on Saturday, maybe we can do it again soon. I won't keep you any longer." He hung up.

It pleased Maggie that Ross had asked to speak to her. Later in the week, he phoned again to see if she could meet him for lunch at the sandwich shop. She was able to get way for thirty minutes, and Carl put a rush on their order. The next evening he called her at her apartment. They chatted for thirty minutes.

...

On Sundays, Maggie customarily drove to church with Caroline and Charlie. They met Lil there, and the foursome sat together. It was quite obvious to everyone that both Caroline and Lil were becoming very fond of Maggie. They had taken the third-row, right-front pew when they first began sitting together. From that week on, no matter what time they arrived, the pew was empty and waiting for them.

Maggie loved Reverend Townlee's preaching, and the folksy way he had of coaxing his congregation to participate in his sermons. Last Sunday, just before the choir sang the opening hymn, Ross had come in the side door from the parking lot and had joined them in their pew. Afterward, they'd all gone back to Lil's for brunch.

Maggie was enjoying all of her newfound friendships. In a short span of time these wonderful people had made her feel a welcome part of this little community. And she loved her job at the clinic. Through it, and the church, she had become acquainted with a large percentage of the population of Serenity. Many were becoming like extended family to her. Often, she found herself thinking and worrying over them even after she went home from the clinic.

Doc and Kathryn were wonderful to work with. Shortly after Maggie had confided in Doc, he had asked her permission to tell Kathryn their secret. He assured Maggie that it would go no further until she was ready to tell the news herself. Maggie suspected that he wanted Kathryn to keep an eye on her and not let her overdo. He also didn't want Maggie exposed to certain illnesses, and if his wife knew Maggie's condition, Kathryn would make sure she was the one to handle those cases.

Today had been a particularly hectic Thursday. Maggie hadn't had a moment to catch her breath. She'd even been forced to drink her morning carton of milk on the run between examining rooms. The last couple of weeks they hadn't been able to close down over the lunch hour, as it seemed everyone in town had an ailment of some sort. They all had staggered their lunches and had eaten on the run, so that they could see patients straight through until closing. At 1:30 P.M. Maggie felt a tap on her shoulder as she drew up a syringe of flu vaccine. She turned to look up into Ross's blue eyes.

"I brought you chicken salad on whole wheat and fresh fruit," he said. "Can you manage a few minutes to sit down and eat with me?"

"Have I ever told how really terrific you are?" she asked with a grin. When she looked at him she noticed his face had flushed. She added, "I'll be with you as soon as I give this injection. And let me guess; I bet you brought a double bacon cheeseburger with fries for yourself."

"Uh, oh," he laughed, "I can see I'm becoming way too predictable. I'll wait for you in the break room."

"Well, you did surprise me by coming, so don't be too hard on yourself," she assured him. She disappeared into examining room two.

Both Maggie and Ross seemed completely oblivious to the raised eyebrows and knowing smiles that were exchanged among Doc, Kathryn and Mildred.

Lunch had been unexpected, and she enjoyed the food as well as the company. She couldn't help but reflect on how very comforting it felt to have a friend with whom you felt so at ease, someone who shared so many of your viewpoints and values. Frequently during her days, she found herself wanting to share with Ross some piece of news she had learned or something that struck her as humorous.

At close to six o'clock that evening, Doc was with his last patient of the day. "You go on home, young lady," he said to Maggie when she stepped into the room to assist him. "Kathryn and I'll finish up here today."

"Thanks, Doc. Room three has been cleaned, and it's all set for tomorrow."

"See you then. Goodnight, Maggie."

She had promised Lil she'd stop by to visit and eat a hamburger with her this evening. Lil had laughingly promised her that it truly would be just the two of them, that they were "ripe for some girl talk."

Maggie knew she couldn't keep putting off sharing the fact that she was pregnant with her friends. Though she wasn't showing any outward signs, she had gained several pounds evenly distributed over her tall, slender frame. And for her tummy, it was only a matter of time now. Maggie had decided that tonight she'd tell Lil after they caught up on the news of the day. When she left there, she'd stop by to tell Caroline and Charlie before going up to her apartment. She didn't want anyone to feel slighted, so she'd make a point to tell all three friends on the same evening.

Then, there was the matter of Ross. What would he think of her when he found out? Would he lose respect for her? Would he still want to be her friend? She certainly hoped so. She'd really miss him if he were no longer a part of her life.

...

Lil had the burgers in the skillet ready to turn on, when Maggie arrived. There was a large bowl of tossed salad on the table, and the fresh apple pie on the counter smelled so good it literally made Maggie's mouth water.

"It's great not to have to go home and cook. I like being pampered."

Lil chuckled, "Have I told you how nice it is to have someone to fuss over? I never did like eating alone."

Maggie stepped to the silverware drawer and got out service for each of them. She took two plates and salad bowls out of the cupboard and put them on the kitchen table.

"Ross stopped by the clinic with lunch, today," she told Lil as she folded two paper napkins and placed one under each fork.

"I know," Lil replied. "I heard him call his order in to Carl, and I figured that's where he was headed. Your name pops into his conversation pretty much every day now. It's Maggie says this, or Maggie thinks that. I'd say you two are becoming pretty good friends." Lil turned to face Maggie. "It must agree with you too, 'cause you've taken on a glow about you of late."

Maggie didn't miss a beat. "We're friends, Lil. Only that." She immediately changed the.subject. "We sure have been busy at the clinic the last few weeks. I think everyone in town has been in sometime during the past month. Prescription receipts must be hitting an all time high down at the drugstore."

Lil let it drop. They had finished eating and were clearing the table when the doorbell rang. Lil looked puzzled. Wiping her hands on her apron, she went to answer it.

"I swear I didn't invite anyone over, Maggie. I don't know who would be coming here at this time of night."

Maggie leaned against the kitchen doorframe as Lil unlatched the front door and pulled it open. The man standing there was of average height, perhaps six feet tall. Maggie thought the stranger relatively good looking. He had a trim build, sun-tanned complexion and light-brown hair.

"Can I help you?" Lil asked looking up at the young man.

"Don't you know me?" he asked.

"Should I?"

"Aunt Lil, it's me!" The man looked down at her and flashed a smile. "I'm your nephew Kevin! Kevin Williams."

Chapter Ten

Lil drew in her breath, "Good Lord, have mercy!" she exclaimed. "It really is you, isn't it?"

Lil took a step forward and pulled him to her patting his broad shoulders with both of her hands. After a moment, she stepped back still holding his arms.

"Let me have a look at you, young man. Hasn't a day gone by since you left, that I didn't ask the good Lord to keep you safe and bring you back to me in His time."

"Aunt Lil, you don't know how many times I've thought about you and wanted to call. I should have let you know that I was fine. But, somehow..."

Maggie stepped into the living room.

"Lil, it's late. You two have lots of catching up to do. I need to leave. I'll call you tomorrow."

"No, Maggie. Please stay for a while. I want you to meet Kevin. I'll put on a pot of green tea." Without waiting for Maggie's answer, she turned to Kevin. "Have you eaten dinner, son?" she asked, already heading for the kitchen.

"I have, Aunt Lil, but hot tea sounds good. I remember how you always loved it."

"Well, you can't say no to my apple Pie, Kev," she told him as she reached up and took a plate from the cupboard for him. "Kevin, this is my good friend Maggie Thornton. She's a nurse for Doc down at the clinic."

"I remember Doc," he said, extending his hand to Maggie. "Hello, Maggie, I'm happy to meet you." He continued to hold her hand. "I think I feel a fever coming on." He smiled as he looked into her eyes. "And you're right, Aunt Lil. I can't say no to a piece of your apple pie," he said, his eyes still fixed on Maggie.

"It's nice to meet you, Kevin." Maggie felt her face flush as she drew her hand back. *Oh spare me that old line.* She felt an instant mistrust of him. Something about his eyes, and the way he looked at her, made Maggie feel very uncomfortable. She really wanted to leave but, for Lil's sake, she took a seat at the table once again.

"Just for a few minutes. It really is getting late."

Kevin joined Maggie at the kitchen table. Lil served his pie and poured their tea, then sat down.

"Now, Kevin, I want to know everything about you since you left here. Are you married? Do you have a family? My goodness, son, you must be what now, close to thirty?"

"No. No. And yes," he replied before popping a big bite of pie into his mouth. "Mmmm, even better than I remembered, Aunt Lil."

She flashed him a toothy grin. "There's another piece right over there with your name on it when that one's gone, Kev. Now, tell me what you've been up to."

"I guess the best place to start, is why I left." He leaned back in his chair and put his fork down before continuing. "I could see how tough it was on you around here with Uncle Henry's drinking, and the constant arguing. I seemed to be a lot of Uncle Henry's problem, so I decided to remove myself from the scene. I thought if I left, maybe it would make things a little easier on you."

"But Kevin, I worried about you so. We had the police and the SBI out lookin' for you and still no trace," she shook her head.

"I know. But I was such a kid and desperate to get away from Henry. I hitched a ride with a trucker as far as Richmond."

"Oh, Kev," Lil exclaimed, "you coudda' been killed."

"I know, Aunt Lil. But I wasn't. He was a really nice fellow, had three kids of his own. When he left me at a gas station in Richmond, I met a family who was on their way to Williamsburg. They took me with them. I got a job there, at Busch Gardens.

"That was the best thing that ever happened to me, because, I met this really nice kid, Grant, who was working there for the summer. We became good friends and he took me home with him to meet his family. When I told them I had lost my mom and was on my own, they insisted I move in with them. They sort of adopted me, figuratively, not legally. His parents were great; they treated me like one of their own. Grant's dad was an attorney, Brad Warren, the senior partner in Warren, Kent, and Crosley. When it came time for Grant to go to College, his father enrolled me too. We both went to William and Mary. Then he sent me to law school at Duke and Grant finished up at MIT. He's a genetic engineer now. And, I'm a tax attorney with a big law firm in Raleigh. We have a lot of clients in the Research Triangle as well as other parts of North Carolina and Virginia."

Lil smiled and shook her head. "I can't get over it, Kev. You bein' all grown up and a big city attorney to boot. I should guess that was one lucky stop you made, and I sure would like to meet them Warrens and tell 'em thanks for being so good to you." She reached across the table and took his hand.

"You can, Aunt Lil. I'll take you up to meet them next time I go for a visit."

"I'd like that, Kev. I really would." Lil beamed at him.

"Anyhow," Kevin went on, "Jes Stanton, the editor of your newspaper, brought his family up to Busch Gardens that summer. We ran into each other. After that, we were in touch from time to time. He's a good man, and I knew he'd hold what I told him in confidence. I knew when Henry died. I also knew you were doing fine. I know I should have come back before, or at least called. I don't have an excuse, but I 'm sorry for all the worry I caused you."

"You know, Jes always did tell me he had a strong feeling you were safe, and that your life was goin fine," Lil affirmed. "Course, I always thought he was just trying to put my mind at ease. How long can you stay, Kevin?"

"I need to get back to Raleigh tomorrow afternoon." He looked at Maggie.

"I plan to visit again soon, maybe stay a little longer next time I come."

Maggie finished her tea. She stood, "I really need to leave, it's been a long day for me, and tomorrow is another work day. It was nice to meet you Kevin," she smiled at him, "and I'm happy for you, Lil." She patted the older woman's shoulder as she passed her and headed for the door.

"I'll see you out, Maggie." Lil stood.

"You stay right here. I know my way out." She left them in the kitchen and walked to the front door.

As she turned the knob, she heard Kevin's voice. "What a looker, that Maggie. Tell me more about her, Aunt Lil."

Not wanting to eavesdrop, Maggie quickly exited the house and hurried to her car. Kevin's arrival had changed her plan of confiding in Lil, perhaps for the best. Maybe she would tell Ross first and see how he reacted before telling the others.

It was nearly ten-thirty when she stopped outside her door and fumbled for the key. She could hear her phone ringing. But, by the time she unlocked the door and reached the phone, it had stopped. She lifted the receiver anyway and was not surprised to hear a dial tone. Maggie wondered if it had been Ross. She contemplated calling him but decided against it. If he hadn't been the caller she wouldn't risk waking him.

...

Sunday morning, Maggie, Caroline and Charlie arrived earlier than usual for the church service. Lil was already in their pew and was all smiles.

"I could hardly wait for you all to get here," she said excitedly. Then she launched into her tale of Kevin's return.

Caroline and Charlie looked surprised. Caroline asked, "Why didn't you tell us, Maggie?"

She laughed, "Why would I do that and deprive Lil of all this pleasure?"

Even the people behind them laughed. "Thanks, Maggie. And it sure is a pleasure." She was in the midst of telling them that Kevin had been quite impressed with Maggie and had asked her to invite Maggie to dinner the next time he visited, when Ross came in the side door and sat down next to Lil.

"Oh Ross," Lil exclaimed excitedly, "Kevin's back! He was here. He spent the night Thursday and actually ended up stayin' over 'til yesterday afternoon. That's why I called and asked Patsy to cover for me. I didn't tell her why, cause I wanted to tell you about it myself."

"Kevin!" Ross' eyebrows shot up. "Hmm, and after all this time. How is he?"

Lil picked up her story with Kevin's interest in Maggie. Maggie was acutely aware of Ross's eyes riveted on her.

...

The week that followed was extremely busy at the clinic. Maggie went in thirty minutes early each morning and was never able to leave before six in the evening. On Thursday, it was after seven before she got away. She and Ross had spoken only briefly a couple of times, and he hadn't called her to have lunch at all. She guessed he knew how busy they were at the clinic by the perscriptions that he was filling down at the pharmacy.

...

By Thursday evening, Maggie was exhausted. When she got home, she fixed herself a hot meal. She filled her bathtub with warm water, made herself a cup of decaffienated green tea and took it into the bathroom with her. She luxuriated in the tub until the water became too cool to be comfortable any longer. Then she went straight to bed.

She fell asleep immediately. She was roused by the shrill ring of her phone. She sat up and rubbed her eyes. *Now who could that be*? She wondered as she stepped onto the floor and went to answer it.

"Maggie." It was Lil's voice. "I was about to give up on you, girl. You weren't in bed, were you?"

"As a matter of fact I was, Lil. What time is it?"

"It's only nine-fifteen, honey. I'm sorry I woke you, and I'm not gonna keep you. I just called to ask you to dinner for your birthday tomorrow night."

"Oh, my gosh." Maggie chuckled. "I'd completely forgotten my birthday. But how did you find out?"

"I have my ways," Lil returned. "Anyway, I've invited Caroline and Charlie, too. Why don't you all come about eight tomorrow night?"

"Lil, that's so sweet of you. It sounds wonderful. Thanks"

"Now, you get on back to sleep," Lil said in a motherly tone. "I'm sorry I woke you. See you tomorrow."

"Thanks," Maggie said. "Night."

She got back into bed. She knew what she had to do. She had to tell these people about the baby, and tomorrow after dinner when they were all together, she would. Then, she'd tell Ross. She rehearsed it mentally a couple of times before falling asleep again.

…

It looked as if they'd finish up early on Friday. At 4:30, Doc told Maggie she could leave. "It'll make up for the long hours you put in during the earlier part of the week. Have a good weekend, and get some rest. We'll see you on Monday."

…

Maggie stopped in to talk to Caroline before she went upstairs to get ready for dinner.

"Happy birthday, Maggie." Caroline hugged her and kissed her cheek. "How many is it? Twenty five, twenty six?"

"You're very kind. Today, I turn thirty; that's why I have to chuckle when Charlie calls me 'little girl'".

"That's young to us. You're still a little girl to him." She smiled at Maggie then grew more serious. "Our Joy would have been twenty-five next month," she said in a near whisper. Then, sounding more upbeat, "I'm so glad you're here, dear, and that the four of us will celebrate together tonight. My goodness, where does the time get to?"

"That's what I've been asking myself these past weeks, Caroline."

"You ride with Charlie and me tonight, honey. We'll leave about seven-fifty. Just come on down when you get ready."

"See you then," Maggie said as she started for the back door. When she reached her apartment, she found a bouquet of crimson roses from the local florist sitting beside the door. She reached for the card and read it. They were from Michael. She left them on the stoop and hurried upstairs.

...

At seven-forty-five, Maggie took a final look at herself in the dresser mirror. She had decided on a pair of kelly green slacks and a cream colored pull over. The slacks had an elasticised waistband, making them one of the more comfortable choices in her wardrobe these days. She fastened the gold locket her mother had given her on her twenty-first birthday around her neck and chose gold dangling-heart earrings. Her hair was finally long enough to put up on her head. She gave the little tendrils that hung down on either side of her face a twist with her fingers then separated her bangs with an Efalock to give them a wispy look. She gave her hair a quick once over with hair spray and checked herself in the mirror. She was pleased. No one would look at her and think she looked four-plus months pregnant. Height certainly had its advantages.

When she reached the bottom step, Charlie and Caroline stepped through their back door. "My, don't you look pretty, little girl!" Charlie said with a grin that spread from one ear to the other.

Caroline was all smiles too. She carried a large box wrapped in lavender and blue birthday paper and tied with purple curling ribbon. "This is for you, but you have to wait 'til after dinner to open it," she said, still grinning.

...

Lil cooked another delicious meal; ham, sweet potatoes, fried okra, and homemade biscuits. She must have made four dozen biscuits.

"When I bake, sometimes I go a little overboard. But it's a big ham, so it'll make good ham biscuits. You all can take some home if there's any left."

Maggie rolled her eyes, "If there isn't any left, we'll all

end up in the emergency room."

Caroline and Charlie looked at Lil, and Charlie gave her a little wink. They had finished the meal and were starting to clear the dishes when they heard a commotion out in front of Lil's house.

"Maggie, would you mind checkin' on that for me?" Lil asked in the midst of taking a handful of dishes to the sink.

"Sure." Maggie reached the front door and opened it. There, huddled on the front porch, stood Doc, Kathryn, Mildred, Carl Lawson and his wife Irene, from the sandwich shop, Bobby Hensley, with his parents, and Ross.

"Happy Birthday, Maggie!" They shouted in unison.

Then, as Maggie looked on, eyes wide with surprise, they burst into a rousing rendition of *Happy Birthday* in at least four different keys. Somehow, they managed to end up all together and on the same note.

"I'm speechless!" Maggie exclaimed.

"That'll be the day!" Doc said good-naturedly.

Maggie leaned down. "And there's my boy, Bobby."

Bobby ran into her arms. "Happy birthday, Nurse Maggie." He planted a big kiss on her cheek.

"I'm so glad you came, too." She kissed him back.

With a grin, he turned to his parents and held out his hand. Sarah Hensley produced a manila folder from behind her back and handed it to Bobby. It was tied with red yarn. With great pride, Bobby offered it to Maggie. "It's for you. I made it for your birthday."

By now, everyone had gathered around Maggie. "Thank you, Bobby. You made it for me? I wonder what it can be," she said, unfastening the yarn.

"It's a..."

"Shhhh, Bobby," Sarah coaxed. "Let Nurse Maggie open it and see for herself."

Maggie lifted the front of the folder, and there was no mistaking as to what the picture was.

"A black widow spider!" Maggie exclaimed.

It was a watercolor painting and very accurate. At the bottom of the picture, the boy had scrawled his name in bold black lettering.

"Bobby. This is excellent! Thank you! On Monday I'm going to frame this, and I think I'll hang it at the office so everyone who comes in can see what a wonderful artist you are."

"Good idea," Doc put in. "That's a fine picture, Bobby."

Bobby beamed with pride. "Welcome," he said shyly casting his eyes toward his feet.

Ross stepped up to Maggie as the others passed Bobby's gift among them. "Happy Birthday, Maggie," he said quietly. "I think your young admirer has just stolen the show. Kids and dogs," he added, chuckling.

The doorbell rang. Doc looked toward the door then back over the group that had gathered. "Who's late? I thought we were all here." He went to the door and opened it.

Kevin Williams peered back at him through an armload of roses. He stepped into the room and over to Maggie. "These are for you, birthday girl. I hope I'm not too late." Maggie looked stunned!

Chapter Eleven

The room hushed for a moment. Even Lil's surprise looked genuine. Doc broke the silence by stepping up to Kevin. "I'm Doc Miller. Do you remember me, Kevin?"

"I do. Good to see you again." Kevin shook Doc's hand.

The others followed Doc's lead. Those who didn't know Kevin introduced themselves. Lil introduced Ross.

"This is my boss, Kevin. And he's a treasure. Best man I ever worked for, bar none."

"Don't let her kid you, Kevin." Ross took Kevin's outstretched hand. "And, I'm the boss as long as I do things Lil's way."

"Come on out to the kitchen everyone, and get yourselves something to munch on," Lil invited. "Now you know why all that ham and biscuits," she said, turning to Maggie. "Dig in folks, we've got cake and ice cream, too!"

Maggie noticed that Ross's demeanor had become considerably more reticent since Kevin's arrival. After the crowd had made the trek through the kitchen and everyone was milling around the living room eating and chatting once again, Maggie found herself in the company of both Ross and Kevin. A few minutes later she excused herself to visit with Carl and Irene. It wasn't long until Kevin had worked his way through the guests to Maggie, Carl and Irene. Within seconds, Ross joined them.

As Kevin relayed how he had ended up in Williamsburg and later in Law School, Ross interrupted. "How could you have been so thoughtless of Lil all these years? Once you knew Henry was no longer in the picture, why didn't you contact her?"

Kevin looked stunned but was at a loss for words for only a moment. "Well, Ross, none of us is perfect. And, yes. It was thoughtless, but I've told Aunt Lil how sorry I am. And, I do intend to make it up to her. I'm going to spend as much time as I can with her now. Thanks for bringing it to my attention here and now though."

Now, words failed Ross. His face flushed. To relieve the tension, Irene made small talk, and Maggie joined in. Maggie was surprised and a bit curious at Ross's behavior. It seemed so out of character for him. Perhaps Lil had told him more of the situation than she'd told Maggie. Maybe he was just feeling protective of this woman who was a very close friend.

Within moments, Ross excused himself and joined another group, but his eyes kept returning to Maggie, Kevin and the Lawsons.

Several had brought gifts for Maggie and, as she opened them, she graciously thanked each. The last package in the pile was from Caroline and Charlie. When she removed the gift-wrapping and lifted the lid, she drew in her breath. It was an exquisite hand made quilt in delicate pastels. Caroline had embroidered her initials into the one of the corners and had dated it today, Maggie's birthday.

Touched, Maggie hugged its softness against her, and her eyes moistened. "Thank you," was all she could manage.

But, her reaction left no doubt in anyone's mind as to how Caroline's offering had moved her.

Across the room, Maggie saw Ross approach Kevin and speak to him briefly. Then he joined Maggie. "I'll say goodnight now, Maggie."

He stood looking at her for a moment, and she thought that his eyes looked as melancholy as they had the first time she'd met him. It saddened her.

"I'm sorry I was rude to Kevin. I don't know why I said what I did to him. I was out of line. I've apologized to him, and I'm apologizing to you, too."

"Don't worry about it. It's forgotten. I'm so glad you were part of my surprise party, Ross. Thanks for coming."

He stood looking down at her, and she found his expression quite poignant. Then, as Ross turned from her and left the party, another pang of sadness swept through Maggie.

...

Ross's departure had started the exodus, and, within ten minutes, most of the other guests had left. Caroline leaned toward Maggie and whispered, "My dear, you look exhausted. Charlie and I are ready to leave whenever you are."

Maggie was suddenly aware of how right Caroline was. "I am tired. I guess it's all this excitement. I'm ready now."

They Thanked Lil and said their good-byes. That left only Kevin with his aunt. Charlie had made a prior trip to the car with the gifts, so Maggie had only the roses to carry with her. Kevin and Lil walked to the door with them.

"I hope to see you next time I'm in town, Maggie," Kevin told her." Even though I had to crash your party, I'm glad I didn't miss it."

"Thanks, Kevin. I never did find out how you knew about this surprise party."

Lil looked questioningly at Kevin awaiting his answer.

He ignored Maggie's query. "I hope you'll enjoy the roses," he called out as Maggie, Charlie and Caroline descended the porch steps.

His attention still made Maggie feel uncomfortable. She didn't want to hurt his feelings, but she wasn't interested in any kind of involvement if that was what he had in mind. She certainly didn't want to encourage him. She probably should have a hear- to-heart with Lil. Or perhaps the situation would take care of itself when she made her announcement. He'd most likely scramble for the bushes then. It was different with Ross. She was completely at ease with him. There was no pressure there; they were coming from the same place, and to each other they were the friend they needed.

Charlie opened the car doors as she and Caroline approached. As she leaned down to get into the back seat, Maggie noticed Ross's car parked across the street. He opened his door and stepped out.

"Maggie," he called. "I waited for you. Could I talk to you please? If it's alright with you, I'll drive you home."

Maggie didn't respond immediately.

Without hesitation Caroline said, "Go on if you want to, honey. We'll take your things in for you."

"Thanks."

Maggie handed Caroline the roses and walked over to Ross's car. He went around and opened the door for her. As she got in, she glanced back at Lil's house and saw Kevin watching them from the window. Ross, no doubt, had noticed too as he walked back to his side of the car and got in.

"Do you feel as if our every move is being scrutinized?" He mumbled.

She let his comment pass without reply.

Ross pulled his silver Buick Electra down the street far enough that he was sure they'd be undetected then parked and turned the engine off.

"I have a little gift for you, but I wanted to give it to

you without the crowd." He handed her a small rectangular package. It was rather clumsily wrapped in blue and tied with white curling ribbon in a single bow.

"Thanks, Ross."

"I'm not much good at gift-wrapping," he told her as she began to open it.

She laughed. "Oh, Ross, I love it!" she exclaimed as she unfolded the last double flap of paper revealing a DVD of *You've Got Mail.* "I only have one problem with this."

"You don't like re-runs?" he asked.

"No. I love re-runs. I don't have a DVD player, so I won't be able to watch it."

"That's not a problem. You can bring it out to my place. How about tomorrow night? I'll cook dinner for us."

"That sounds great!" She noticed that his eyes had brightened.

"I have to warn you though, I cook only a little better than I gift wrap."

"I'm not worried. I'll help with dinner. Four hands should make it at least twice as good.

"No way am I going to turn that offer down. "

"Can I bring anything?"

"Only yourself. I make pretty good spaghetti. I'll fix that and a salad, if it sounds good to you."

"Sounds great."

"I'll get everything. I have a bottle of wine I've been saving for a special occasion. We can open that."

"Let me bring some vegetables from Charlie's garden. They're going to spoil if I don't quit eating out, and no wine for me," she added quickly. "I'm strictly a teetotaler, milk to be more exact. But, I'll have it in a wine glass, and I'll drink a toast with you."

That made him laugh. "Why not?"

She was acutely aware of how comforting it was to hear him laughing again. He started the car and drove her home.

He parked right outside her door and waited until she waved at him from her window before he pulled away.

Maggie let the curtain fall as Ross drove away. She went into her bedroom. She felt tired, but she wasn't sleepy after she got ready for bed. She decided to slip into her robe and listen to a tape. She and Ross had stopped in at a Founder's Day celebration in Fayetteville a while back, and there was a young entertainer performing, Brad Alan. He sang, his group playing his original music, and they had thoroughly enjoyed his show. Afterward Ross bought one of his tapes for her. A few days after that, she turned the radio on and recognized his voice. The Fayetteville station was playing one of his recordings.

She started over to turn the tape player on, but, before she reached it, her phone rang. She had half-a-mind to let it ring, but her curiosity got the best of her. Whoever it was, they were persistent. She lifted the receiver on the seventh ring.

"Hello."

"Maggie, please don't hang up."

It was Michael! What on earth could he want? Her stomach started doing flip-flops.

"I couldn't let your birthday pass without calling to see how you are and to wish you happy birthday. Did you get my flowers?"

Now as before, when he had shown up at her door, she struggled to keep the timbre of her voice steady.

"I did. Thank you, Michael. But you shouldn't have sent them." she said icily.

"Brrrrrr. Give me a minute to run get my overcoat," he said. He laughed a nervous laugh. "I don't blame you, Maggie. I wish I could undo everything that's happened these past months."

"For some things, there are no second chances, Michael." She could see his face in her mind's eye, and she could picture that little boy expression he must be wearing. It had served him so well in the past. "Good-bye, Michael."

"Wait! Please. Just give me a minute." He persisted.

Maggie remained on the line.

"I feel like we *do* have a second chance on this one, Maggie. Robyn isn't pregnant. It was a false positive...on the pregnancy test that she did. In fact, I think she lied to me from the start. I don't think she ever did a test. Anyway, it's over between us. So, we were lucky this time. And you and I deserve to give us a second chance. I still love you, Maggie, darling, and I miss you so much. Nothing's the same without you."

Maggie felt nauseated. She had to get off the phone. "I can't talk now, Michael. But, no! We can't try again. I—I have to go now. Please, don't call me again."

"I'm coming to see you, Maggie. We have to talk face to face. I know I can change your mind. I've got tomorrow off, don't have to be back 'til Sunday afternoon."

"No!" she snapped. "Don't do that! I won't be here. I'm leaving town in the morning. I'm going to visit my aunt," she lied. "Good bye." She slammed the receiver down and dashed for the bathroom. She barely made it before she lost her birthday dinner.

Afterward, she began to sob. Why did he have to call, why couldn't he just leave her alone? Why did he have to intrude himself in her life tonight and spoil a perfectly lovely birthday? She had reached the point of being able to go for several days at a time without thinking of how he had hurt her. Now, he was trying to undo it all. And damn, even with the rotten thing he'd done to her, when she heard his voice and pictured his face, she went all mushy inside. "What on earth is wrong with you, girl?" she asked aloud.

She splashed cold water on her face and looked at herself in the mirror. She took a jar of night cream out of her medicine cabinet and smoothed it over her face and neck.

She decided not to answer her phone the rest of the weekend. Her first order of business on Monday morning would be to call the phone company and ask for an unlisted number.

And, she couldn't take a chance on Michael showing up here and having to face him again. She would talk to Caroline and Charlie in the morning and ask them to say she was gone if Michael should show up asking for her. That wouldn't be a lie; she would be gone from the apartment. She'd have to park her car elsewhere, and she would stay away from the house for most of the day. Then she'd be at Ross's tomorrow evening. That left only Sunday morning to worry about. She could spend the day with Lil. Michael would have to be back at the hospital sometime Sunday afternoon. Why, oh why, couldn't he just leave her alone? The break had been made; why didn't he just get on with his life?

"Oh, dear God, please don't let him show up here," she whispered.

Chapter Twelve

Maggie managed to stay away from her apartment for the entire day Saturday. She stopped by the drugstore around three in the afternoon. Both Ross and Lil were working. They staggered Saturdays off, but both worked every other weekend together, and Ross was always on-call during his off time. He carried a beeper so that if an emergency occurred he could respond, but it wasn't often that such an occasion arose. Maggie decided it was one of the unique perks of living in a small town.

"What brings you by this afternoon?" Lil wanted to know. "You're not sick are you? You look a little peaked."

"No, I'm not sick. I just can't go home." She told Lil about Michael's call. Maggie had told her a little about Michael soon after they had become acquainted. She hadn't gone into the sordid details, but the older woman knew enough that she would certainly help in any way she could to prevent him from finding Maggie.

Ross caught Maggie's eye from the pharmacy at the back

of the store and waved. "We're still on for tonight, aren't we?" he called.

"We are," she called back.

"I'll pick you up around six. I have a couple more things to do here, and then we're going to close up. We haven't had a soul in since lunch, except you."

Maggie walked part way back to the pharmacy. "Let me drive over. I don't want my car at the apartment tonight. I'll tell you about it when I get there."

Ross looked a little puzzled. "Okay. If you're sure, but I don't want you driving home alone at night, even in Serenity. I don't live just around the corner like Lil does, you know. I'll follow you back to town. Are you sure you can find your way out?"

"I've got a pretty good idea. Would you mind jotting down the landmarks?" Ross lived several miles from town in the county. He had told her a little about his place, but she'd never been there.

"I'll draw her a map, Ross. You finish up what you're doin' there."

"Thanks."

Before she left the drugstore, Maggie called Caroline. "Any sign of Michael?" she asked.

"Not even a hair. Charlie's stayed out in the garden most of the day. He'd know if Michael even rode by."

"I'm coming home just long enough to change clothes, and then I'm going to Ross's for dinner," Maggie told her. "I'm going to leave my car around the corner."

"You go on and pull it into our garage and close the door. Charlie has ours on the street."

...

At 5:45, Maggie started out the door and was half way down the steps before she remembered the video and had to go back.

By the time she was actually on her way, she was beginning to have a feel for what it's like to be a fugitive, constantly looking over one's shoulder and paranoid about one's every move. It would be good to get away from town tonight and spend the evening in the country with Ross. She went into the garage and got into her car. Once out on the road, she turned right on Main St., then headed out of town

Fifteen minutes later, she was still driving. "I should be getting close."

She was looking for a sign that read "Groves Picnic Shelter", and she hadn't seen it yet. She drove on a bit further and came upon the Revival Baptist Church. "Oh, oh," she said aloud. "You've gone too far, girl." She turned into the church parking lot and opened the map that Lil had drawn for her. It didn't appear she'd overshot it by much. When she headed back there was no traffic behind her, and she was able to drive more slowly. When she did spot the landmark, she understood why she had missed it. It was a small, rusted sign with black lettering, and the sign had been bent in the opposite direction of the turn.

She drove a quarter of a mile down the rutted gravel road through a dense growth of trees, waist-high grass and weeds and patchy, light fog. *This could be creepy in the dark*, she thought to herself, *and it seems so desolate*. She was glad Ross had said he'd follow her home. She couldn't help wondering what the attraction of this place was for him.

She bumped along for a minute more before going up a slight incline. At the top was a clearing. Then Maggie understood what had brought Ross out here.

Beyond her lay one of the most spectacularly beautiful settings Maggie had ever laid eyes on. Nestled among stately oak trees flaunting all the glorious colors of late October, stood an old two-story gray frame home. It had green shutters and an inviting front porch that rambled across the entire front of the house, down one side and around to the back. Smoke rose from the brick chimney and drifted over the peaceful rivulet to the right of the dwelling then spiraled upward until it became one with the billowing clouds. Autumn wild flowers dotted the water bank, and their reflections mingled with the majestic old trees to create a rainbow of fall colors on the silky water. Through the distant mist, Maggie could make out a graceful bridge arching across the narrowest part of the brook. A rowboat, moored at the end of a wooden dock to the side of the house, swayed ever so lightly in the softly rippling water.

As Maggie parked the car and turned off the motor, Ross opened one of the small-paned double doors and stepped onto the front porch.

"Maggie," he called. Welcome to…"

"Paradise," she finished the sentence for him.

"So, you like my old cabin in the woods, do you?" He looked very pleased as he reached her car and opened her door.

She grabbed the bag of vegetables from the back seat, picked up the video and got out.

"Let me take those," Ross said, reaching for her bag. "Come on in. I'll just deposit these in the kitchen."

"Let me look around out here before I go in. This place is absolutely wonderful! It takes my breath away. Why didn't you tell me how phenomenal it is?"

"I know how I feel about it, but not everyone views it as I do," he said pensively.

She knew exactly who he was referring to. She walked to the water's edge and stooped to smell the flowers. "I'll have to admit, some of them look lots prettier than they smell."

"You're right about that. That's why they stay outside on the riverbank. What do you think of my bridge?" he asked, gesturing downstream.

"You're kidding, aren't you? You didn't really build it, did you?"

"Not alone. Seth from the hardware store helped me. Doc helped some, too, on the weekends. It took us a few weeks to finish, but it was good therapy for me."

"How do you keep up with this place? It's so large."

"I have the upstairs rooms closed off, now. I live downstairs. I had hoped to fill the upstairs with kids, but things don't always turn out like we want them to, do they?"

"No. They certainly don't." She tucked her hands into her pockets and continued walking. "How did you ever find this place?"

"I didn't. It found me. It belonged to my grandparents. I spent all my summers here with them. I fished in that pond every day of every summer, and I helped my grandpa around the house and yard. They knew how much it meant to me, and, after my grandma died, my granddad told me he had put in his will that it was to be mine when he was gone. He died during my last year in college, and, when Melanie and I were married shortly after graduation, we moved out here. She never did see in it what I did."

Maggie didn't comment. She started around to the back of the house. "You have your own vegetable garden, don't you?"

"I sure do. When you leave, you can take enough with you to restock what you brought with you tonight."

"Between you and Charlie, I just might sprout pink ears and turn into a rabbit. I will take a few things home with me, see what kind of a farmer you are."

They walked back around to the front of the house and started up the steps. "Some Saturday, when you aren't working, I'd love to go out in that boat and fish with you. I loved it as a child, too. I haven't been in years."

He opened the front door for her, and she stepped into his huge living room. The ceilings were so high, at least twelve feet, Maggie thought; they made the rooms appear even more expansive. The furniture, two massive brown leather sofas and two beige Lazy Boy recliners, looked comfortably masculine. The whole place had an ambiance of quiet strength that so personified Ross. Standing here, Maggie felt both safe and comfortable. A heavy oak coffee table was centered between the sofas, and a big screen TV stood at the far end of the room. A cozy fire crackled in the large, red-brick fireplace. Beyond the living room stretched a formal dining room furnished in antique cherry. The room looked spacious, even with a table and eight chairs, a hutch and buffet. She supposed that the furniture had belonged to his grandparents. The kitchen was at the back of the house.

"Your home is wonderful inside as well as out. "

"It's comfortable," he said with a smile, obviously pleased at her approval.

As they got closer to the kitchen, the aroma of the spaghetti sauce grew stronger.

"Hmmm, I'm just beginning to realize how hungry I am," Maggie told him. "Is that a combination of curry and green pepper I'm smelling?"

"Among other things."

The kitchen definitely had the look of a male cook. Bowls in need of rinsing, and pans, dishes and several glasses cluttering the counter tops. A soup kettle filled with the spaghetti sauce and meatballs steamed away on the stove. It had obviously been boiling for some time and had splattered about the range top. Maggie smiled and shook her head as she surveyed the mess. *All men are alike in the kitchen*, she thought to herself as she remembered her father and grandfather's forays in cooking.

Ross picked up a long, wooden-handled spoon and began stirring his creation.

"I'll grab a sponge and start the clean-up," Maggie offered.

A few minutes later the kitchen was relatively neat, the dirty dishes had been put in the dishwasher, and they set about chopping and dicing the fresh vegetables Maggie had brought for the salad. Within thirty minutes of Maggie's arrival, they were ready to sit down to their meal.

"Would you like to eat in the dining room or the kitchen?"

"I'll leave that up to you; either is fine with me."

Ross got out plates and table service and took them into the dining room. "I don't use this often, so we'll eat in here tonight. He set his place at the head of the table with Maggie to his right. He went to the hutch and removed two smoke-colored, crystal wine goblets. He opened the bottle of Chardonnay he had chilling and filled his glass, then carried Maggie's to the kitchen and filled it with milk.

When they were seated at the table, Maggie raised her goblet. "What shall we drink to?" she asked smiling.

"Well, let me see." He thought a moment. "Let's toast us. You've made an amazing difference in my life, Maggie."

After he said it, Maggie noticed that his face and neck flushed a little.

"The feeling's mutual. You're special to me, Ross," she added softly as their goblets clinked.

Dinner was very tasty. Maggie declined seconds, not because she didn't like it, but because it was fairly spicy, and she knew she'd pay for it during the evening if she indulged herself now.

When the meal was finished and the dishes were out of the way, Ross asked, "Would you like to sit on the front porch for a while before we watch the movie?"

"I'd love to," Maggie said, going into the living room for her sweater.

"I don't know if you'll be warm enough in that. Let me get you one of my jackets to put over it."

He disappeared for a moment and returned wearing a navy flannel pullover and carrying a brown and tan checked fleece jacket for her. She was waiting for him at the front door. He slid the jacket around her shoulders, and his hands lingered for a moment. Maggie felt a strange sensation in the pit of her stomach.

They stayed outside only a few minutes. The temperature was dipping rapidly as is often the case in late October when the days are warm, but the evenings become quite chilly.

"I think we're supposed to get down close to freezing tonight," Ross said, "and the way the temperature's dropping, I think the forecast was on the money this time."

"I agree," Maggie said through chattering teeth. "As much as I love this view and listening to these night sounds, I'm ready to go in," she said rising.

Ross opened the door and put his hand on the small of Maggie's back as they went into the living room. There was that sensation again. She tried to focus on something else.

She walked over and sat down on the sofa that faced the television set.

Ross picked the DVD up off of the coffee table, put it in the player, went back to the sofa and sat down beside Maggie. With a click of the remote the movie began.

Maggie found it as engaging the second time through as she had the first. However, this time she thought she was in better control of her emotions and would escape without the tears. She was wrong. At precisely the same place in the movie, she felt the tears beginning to well in her eyes. She tried to take a deep breath and blink them away to no avail. Ross must have sensed it, for he reached for a Kleenex from the box on the coffee table and handed it to her.

"Are you crying this time too, Maggie?" He asked softly.

"I'm afraid so." She tried to laugh as more tears spilled onto her cheeks.

He reached for another Kleenex, moved a little closer to her and gently dabbed beneath her eyes. "Now that's the sign of a really good movie. You know exactly what's coming, and it gets you anyway."

She looked into his eyes and smiled. Before she realized what was happening, he leaned over and his lips brushed hers. She leaned against his chest. His warm, moist lips covered hers. His arms encircled her.

"Maggie," he whispered, his breath hot against her lips. "Maggie," he whispered again, pulling her even closer.

She returned his kisses as she wrapped her arms about his neck letting her fingers caress the back of his head. Their bodies sank against the sofa pillow until Maggie was lying on top of him. She felt his arousal hard against her; her body responded. Pleasure surged through her. It was intoxicating to lie here in this man's arms.

Quite suddenly, she came to her senses. What was she doing? She was pregnant, with another man's baby! Ross had no idea. She now realized how much she had come to care for him. Her feelings when he touched her earlier this evening were clear to her now. And when he kissed her, both her mind and her body's response to him made it crystal clear. But Ross had been hurt so deeply in the past. How would he react to her reality? She knew she had to tell him. But, not now. No. Now was not the time.

She pulled free of his embrace and rose. "Ross, I have to go. It's nothing you've done. Please understand that. There are things… things that could hurt you." She began to sob.

Ross looked bewildered.

She turned and took a few steps toward the chair and grabbed her sweater.

Ross was on his feet now. "Maggie, I don't understand."

She didn't hesitate. She ran to the door and down the steps. She got into her car. She started the engine, turned around and headed back toward town.

Chapter Thirteen

Maggie's car bumped and bounced down the gravel road through the dense growth back toward the main road. Even when she slowed to a crawl, it seemed a rougher ride than it had when she came. Before she reached the highway, she became aware of headlights behind her.

"Oh, what must you think of me?" she asked aloud. She hoped he would just follow her into town then return home. She needed time to think and sort out how she was going to handle this new situation. Fifteen minutes later she entered Serenity, and Ross continued to follow her.

When she got to her apartment and stopped, he pulled up beside her and turned off his engine. They got out of their cars.

"Maggie, I have to talk to you," he said quietly. "Please, let me come up for a few minutes."

"Please, not tonight. I agree that we need to talk. But, this isn't a good time," she pleaded, looking into his eyes.

"Maggie, please. I promise I won't stay long, but we

can't part like this. I feel I need to explain what happened earlier." He looked so dejected.

She hadn't the heart to refuse him. She unlocked the downstairs door. "Come on, let's talk." She wasn't sure what she was going to say. She had so many feeling to sort out. Suddenly, she felt spent, exhausted.

When they were in the living room, she asked, "Shall I put on some tea? Or, I can offer you a glass of milk?"

"I don't want anything to drink, Maggie. I just want you to sit down and hear me out," he said solemnly, taking a seat on her couch.

She sat down in the easy chair across the room from him.

"I owe you an explanation for my behavior tonight. I've had some time, before tonight, to think about what I'm going to say to you. I know it comes as no surprise to you that our friendship has become extremely important to me. I felt it was mutual. I've considered you trustworthy, and I've told you things I haven't told anyone else. I thought you felt the same about me. I thought that defined our relationship until a wake-up call the night of your surprise party. Well, maybe it started even before that. I guess it began that weekend when Lil said Kevin was interested in you, and I found myself resenting the man without even knowing him. He really got under my skin showing up at the party the way he did, and I had no right to feel that way." Ross's voice was resonant and controlled as he continued.

"I was inexcusably rude to him. But it did start me thinking as to why I acted that way. And the only conclusion I could come to, no matter how many times I thought about it, was that, even though I never intended to, I was beginning to care for you. Tonight, it's so clear to me. Maggie, I'm in love with you."

She sat staring at him silently with tears in her eyes.

"I couldn't help myself tonight when I dried your eyes. I had to kiss you. I'm sorry if I've upset you or if I've done anything to jeopardize our relationship. But I liked kissing you. It felt so very right. And from your response, I thought you liked it too." He looked at her, awaiting her reply.

She had so many things she wanted to tell him. But where, where should she begin? Her mind raced. *Give me the right words*, she prayed silently.

With no response from her, Ross rose slowly. "I'm so sorry, Maggie. I've obviously misinterpreted our whole relationship. I'm sorry if I've hurt you." He started for the door.

Don't let him go like this! Why are you acting like such a coward? Say something, anything. Just don't let him walk out that door now.

She rose to her feet. "Ross, wait. I have so much to tell you; I don't know where to start. Please. Sit back down, and let me try to explain why I ran out like I did tonight."

Without a word, he walked back to the couch. He sat down and waited for her to begin.

Maggie sat down beside him, took a deep breath and shook her head slowly. "It's because, when you kissed me, I did realize how much I care for you. And that is precisely why I ran."

"Then I really don't understand. What are you concerned about? That you can't trust me? I'd never do anything like Michael did. I could never be unfaithful to the woman I love. To you, Maggie."

"No. It's not that. I do trust you. It's that there's a lot about me that you don't know. I should have told you before now. I told you how Michael betrayed me, but I didn't tell you everything. I don't have a right to let myself fall in love with you, Ross." She began to sob.

"I still don't understand. What is it?" he asked leaning forward on the sofa. "Why can't you let yourself love me? Are you…" he hesitated. "Are you and Michael married? Is that why?"

"No. Not married, thank God. It's because I'm pregnant. I'm pregnant with Michael's baby."

Ross' jaw dropped. He stared at her in silence shaking his head slowly.

"See, you do think I'm awful. I've disappointed you. I'm..." she stammered. "I'm so sorry, Ross." Tears flooded down her cheeks.

He leaned toward her. "I am disappointed. I'm so disappointed that you didn't feel you could trust me enough to tell me. That you didn't think our friendship was strong enough that you could confide in me." He took her in his arms and pulled her against him. He held her until she stopped crying.

"Oh, Ross," she murmured against his shoulder, "You're so absolutely wonderful. You're the last person on earth I wanted to hurt. I'm so sorry for all of this."

"I know. I understand. You've been through so much in the last year," he whispered against her hair. He kissed her cheek. "What's Michael's attitude about this?"

"He doesn't know. And I don't want him to."

"This is too much for you be coping with alone. Does anyone else know? Lil or Caroline?"

"No. Only Doc and Kathryn. Doc's taking care of me. I was waiting for the right time to tell the rest of you, and I just never seemed to be able to find it. I knew I couldn't wait much longer. I even thought of leaving, but I have nowhere to go."

"Never do that, Maggie," he tightened his embrace. "Don't even think of it."

The shrill ring of the phone intruded on their privacy. Maggie sat motionless. "Don't you want to see who that is?" Ross asked her.

"No. I'm afraid it might be Michael. I never did get to tell you about his call to me last night." Maggie relayed the details of their phone conversation. Part way into the explanation, the phone stopped ringing.

When she finished, he asked, "How do you feel about his proposal?"

"I could never trust him again. And I can honestly say I don't love him anymore, and now I wonder how I ever could. But I have to be admit that, until a couple of months ago, even after all he'd done to me and the terrible hurt he caused, there were times when I'd hear his voice or just think of him, something inside me longed for the way it was before any of this happened. Wasn't that foolish of me?"

"No. It's perfectly understandable. This is all still pretty fresh with you. It takes time to begin to heal."

"He hurt my pride, and he shook my confidence. I wanted to feel that he was sorry and that he wanted me back. Then, when he actually did, I found that I didn't want him."

"I know," he agreed. "It's damn tough on the ego when someone cheats on you. You have lots of crazy thoughts running through your mind. Believe me, I know."

She realized that at some point in their conversation the phone had stopped ringing. "He can't know about this child," she continued. "God only knows how he might use it to pressure me now that he's decided he wants me back."

"Good point. I think…"

The phone began to ring again. Ross released her, rose and walked to the phone. On the fourth ring he picked up the receiver.

"Hello, " he said quietly. "What number were you calling?" he paused. "You have the number you dialed, but you have the wrong person," he replied looking at Maggie. "No problem." He hung up.

"It was a man. I didn't recognize the voice, but I assume it was Michael. He asked if he had reached Ms. Thornton. You heard what I said. I *am* the wrong person for him to be talking to."

"Thanks." She took a tissue from her pocket and dabbed at her cheeks.

"I've changed my mind," he said suddenly. "I will take that cup of tea if your offer still stands."

"It does," she said, rising and starting into the kitchen. He followed her and sat at the table while the tea brewed.

"I don't know why it took me so long to tell you this, Ross. It wasn't nearly as bad as I thought it would be. My thinking hasn't always been the clearest recently."

"If you like, I'll go with you when you tell Lil and Caroline and Charlie."

"That sounds good to me. I think we should tell them soon. What do you think about after church tomorrow? We can all come back here for lunch."

"Let's plan on it." He smiled at her. All of the strain had disappeared from his face now.

When they had finished their tea, she walked with him to the door. "I'll pick you up at ten-forty-five in the morning." He took her in his arms and held her tightly, his hands caressed her back as his lips found hers.

...

Ross arrived a few minutes early to pick Maggie up for church. When she heard the car pull up she looked out the window and, seeing that it was Ross, she hurried down the stairs. She met him at the lower door.

"I told Caroline and Charlie that we'd see them at church."

He leaned down and kissed her. "And good morning to you, too," he said, a broad smile curving his lips. "I like saying good morning to you like this," he said, stealing another kiss. "I came a little early because I wanted some time to talk before church."

He opened her car door for her then went around to his side and got in, but he didn't start the engine.

She shifted in her seat to face him. "You look tired this morning."

"I didn't sleep much. I couldn't stop thinking about

us. I love you, Maggie, and I want to marry you. I want this baby to be ours."

"I don't know what to say. This is all so new to me."

"I understand. You need some time to think about it. Take as long as you need. But please, just don't say anything until you can say yes. I love you, the pregnancy has nothing to do with it. I want to spend the rest of my life with you, Maggie. I have a big house with lots of empty rooms. I want to fill those rooms with our family."

He leaned over and kissed her with such intensity that it left her feeling weak. "If we don't leave for church soon, we might not get there at all," she told him catching her breath and reaching up to smooth her hair.

...

He started the car, and they headed toward the church. They were both so intent on one another that they failed to notice the man slouched down in the front seat of a black Ford Taurus. It had been strategically parked around the corner affording a clear view of Maggie's apartment. After Ross and Maggie passed the vehicle, the driver straightened himself and started his car. He followed with enough distance between them that he wouldn't be detected.

Chapter Fourteen

Ross parked his car in front of the church instead of at the side as he usually did. Reverend Townlee was at the front door greeting the parishioners as they arrived. Maggie and Ross stopped to chat briefly then went into the sanctuary. When they reached their pew, Maggie went in first and, to her surprise, found Kevin sitting with Lil. Caroline and Charlie hadn't arrived yet. Kevin looked surprised to see Maggie and Ross together.

"It's good to see you again, Maggie," Kevin said, smiling into her eyes. He glanced at Ross and extended his hand. "Hello, Ross," he said coolly.

Caroline and Charlie came in shortly after and took their seats. Almost immediately, the service began. A little over an hour later, the friends walked out of the church together. Maggie had spoken with Caroline and Charlie earlier that morning and had invited them for lunch. She had planned to include Lil before the service as they all usually spent some time together on Sundays. She didn't invite Lil when she found Kevin with her. She didn't want him around when she finally told her friends; she didn't want Lil left out either. She found herself feeling very irritated with Kevin. He always seemed to be butting in. But then, she told herself, she had no right to feel that way. *After all, he is Lil's nephew, and Lil has been so happy since he's come back into her life*. Maggie chided herself for being selfish. She should be happy for Lil. Still, she couldn't help but wish Kevin hadn't come today.

When they descended the church steps, the little group gathered on the front lawn. Kevin spoke first. "I'd like you all to be my guests for lunch. You can name the place," he said, looking at Maggie.

"Thanks," Ross said, "but Maggie and I already have plans."

Kevin ignored Ross. "Maggie, could I talk to you alone for a minute?" he asked, his eyes still fixed on her.

She looked at Ross. "I'll be right back." She stepped aside with Kevin.

When they were out of earshot of the others, Kevin spoke. "I know I keep turning up uninvited, but I'm never quite sure when I'm going to be able to get away from Raleigh. I'd like to see more of you, Maggie. Is it alright with you if I call this week and we plan something for next weekend?"

"I'm flattered, Kevin. But my answer will have to be no. You see, it's become serious between Ross and me."

Kevin's eyebrows shot up. "Oh, really? When did this happen? I thought, that, from what everyone said, you were no more than friends. Does Aunt Lil know?"

"No. She doesn't. We've just realized it ourselves."

"Well, I guess that's that." There was an edge in Kevin's voice. "Ross is lucky. I guess I should have come back sooner. What's that old saying? A day late and a dollar short?" Something snapped between Kevin's fingers but Maggie couldn't discern what as they walked back to join the others.

Caroline and Charlie thanked Kevin but declined his invitation, also. They made no excuse.

"Well, I guess it's just the two of us, Aunt Lil. I can't even seem to give lunch away today." He tried to sound casual, but there was definite irritation in his tone.

The group broke up soon after. As Maggie and Ross got into the car, a stranger got out of a black Ford Taurus that was parked across the street from the church. He crossed over to the church lawn and walked up to Kevin. Maggie saw the stranger's mouth move, then he extended his hand to Kevin. *Curious*, she thought, perhaps someone sent by his law firm with a message for Kevin.

They drove in silence until they were back at the apartment. Before they got out of the car, Ross turned to Maggie, "Well, I have to admit my curiosity has the best of me. Are you going to tell me what Kevin had to say?"

"He wanted to call me this week to make plans for next weekend."

"And?"

"I told him I couldn't."

"Because?" Ross prompted. "You're enjoying this, aren't you?" He laughed.

Maggie chuckled, too. "I guess I am at that. I told him that I was serious about you. That we had both just realized it, and that was why my answer had to be no. That and the fact that he gives me the willies. Of course, I didn't tell him that."

"I thought he looked a bit dejected when you two were finished talking."

"He seemed irritated to me. But I have the feeling that it won't set him back for long," Maggie said. "Kevin strikes me as resilient, if anything." She glanced at her watch. "I need to go upstairs and get lunch ready. I told Caroline and Charlie to come up around 1:00, and that's only fifteen minutes away."

"I'll help," he offered, as they got out of the car and headed upstairs.

...

Lunch was ready when Caroline and Charlie arrived. There was a platter of cold cuts and cheeses, and there were kaiser rolls to make their sandwiches. Maggie had also prepared a large bowl of fresh fruit. "I don't have anything for dessert," she told them. "The fruit will have to do."

Caroline brought a bouquet of cut flowers. Maggie found a vase for them and placed them in the center of the kitchen table.

"Caroline keeps me in fresh flowers. I'm getting spoiled. My table's gonna look awfully bare come this winter."

When they finished eating, Maggie said, "Let's go sit in the living room. Ross and I can do these dishes later. We have something to tell you." She looked at Ross. He nodded and winked at her.

She and Ross sat down on the sofa. Caroline and Charlie took the two remaining chairs and looked quizzically at one another. Before Maggie began, Ross reached over and took her hand.

"I've been trying for some time now to tell you what I'm going to say today. I guess I've been putting it off because I wasn't sure how you'd take it."

Caroline looked as if she were going to cry. Her voice broke, "Maggie, you're scaring me," she said softly.

"No, Caroline. It's nothing for you to be frightened about. It's just that I'm pregnant. I'm going to have a baby."

Caroline jumped out of her seat and ran to Maggie. "I'm so relieved. I was afraid you were going to leave us…to leave Serenity. That's wonderful, wonderful news." Maggie stood, and Caroline hugged her.

"That's great," Charlie said grinning. "I like the idea of a little one about."

Caroline went back to her chair.

"As best we have it figured, I'm closing in on five months now, and it won't be long until you see me in maternity clothes. I'm down to only two pair of slacks that still fit comfortably."

"I thought you were filling out your clothes a little better than you used to," Caroline told her. "But I just thought it was all our dinners and lunches and birthday parties. You look great, Maggie. Being pregnant becomes her, doesn't it, Charlie?"

"That, it does!" he agreed heartily.

Caroline was pensive for a moment. "You know, I thought when we lost Joy and Jason, that we'd missed all the happiness of having a family, of being grandparents. And then you came along, Maggie." Caroline's eyes moistened. "You were special to us right from the start, and you've added so much to our lives and now this. I just can't believe it. It's as if we've been given a second chance."

Maggie was touched. "My baby's going to need loving grandparents. I don't have any family left to give him, or her," she added quickly.

Caroline and Charlie turned their attention to Ross who had been sitting quietly at Maggie's side through all of this. Maggie continued.

"I guess you've figured from the time frame that Michael is the baby's father. And I'm sure you can guess by the way I feel about him that I don't intend for him to find out. He's a chapter in my life story that is closed forever," she said adamantly.

"I met Ross my first day in Serenity, as I met the two of you. He and I became friends almost from the start." She emphasized the almost. She looked at him and smiled. "Now that friendship seems to be intensifying. Ross and I may have another announcement to make very soon."

Caroline grinned at her. "I guess you two were the last ones to realize that, Maggie. Everyone in town saw it before you did."

Ross beamed at them. "Actually, I think Maggie was the last to know; it's been dawning on me for some time now, too. I guess she just needed a little more time to come around to it."

"Maggie's had a way of reaching into all our hearts from the very first day she arrived," Caroline said tenderly. "She's been better for me than all the pills Doc ordered."

"You're absolutely right about that," Ross said ardently.

"Oh, stop. Stop, all of you." Maggie laughed. "You'll give me a big head. Now all I need to do is tell Lil. Then I can put on maternity clothes and let the rest of the town spread the news."

The friends chatted for a few more minutes before Caroline and Charlie left. When they were alone, Ross said, "Come out to my place, and later we can go to dinner somewhere."

"It's been quite a day for me, and I have to admit I'm really tired. I think I'll take a rain check, stay here and make it an early evening. I need a good night's rest. I have a few things that I need to do to get ready for my week. I've been away from the apartment most of the weekend."

"I understand. I'm a little tired myself. Your announcements are tough on me, too. The day went great though, didn't it? And do you know what I thought the best part of it all was?"

"I think I do, but I want to hear you say it," she leaned toward him and tickled his lips with her tongue.

He pulled her against him as she did. "The best part was that you said we might have another announcement soon." He wrapped his arms tightly about her and kissed her, a long, lingering kiss.

When he released her, she felt lightheaded. "You make my head spin," she whispered.

"I love you, Maggie Thornton."

"And I love you, so very much."

"I'll call you later," he told her, kissing her lightly on the forehead, "to say goodnight."

He went out the door and down the steps. She watched from her window as he drove away. Quite unexpectedly, a lonely, empty feeling swept through her. And it struck her how terribly important this extraordinary man had become to her world. Why had it taken her this long to realize just how much he meant to her?

But, there was more than one person to consider now. There was a baby, and that unborn child was now her most important consideration. She mustn't rush into anything. Though she knew how important children were to Ross, she still felt she needed to take her time before making such an important commitment. She must think through every aspect of it.

She busied herself straightening up about her place, then went into her bedroom and changed her bed linens. That was usually one of her Friday night chores, but this weekend her routine had been altered.

When the phone rang a while later, she hurried to answer it, expecting to hear Ross's voice.

"Maggie?" It was a woman. The voice sounded a bit unsteady and high-pitched but vaguely familiar. The woman cleared her throat and spoke again. "Maggie, this is Robyn. Please don't hang up. I've called as a friend... to warn you ...about Michael."

Maggie was shaken. "A friend?" She replied emotionally. "You call me as my friend? Oh, please, Robyn! Spare me."

"Please hear me out, Maggie. I'm trying to help you."

Maggie sighed, "Okay, Just tell me whatever it is you have to say so we can end this once and for all."

"I don't blame you for the way you feel. I'm not going to make any excuses; there are none. But you can take this for what it's worth; I did you a damn big favor. Michael can't be faithful to anyone. I wasn't the first woman he cheated on you with. And he wasn't faithful to me either in the short time we were together."

"What can you expect?" Maggie asked coolly.

"I know, you're right. You can't tell me anything I haven't already told myself a hundred times, Maggie."

"Michael called here a couple of nights ago and said you weren't pregnant. He said it was a false positive on the pregnancy test, so I guess you're fortunate in that way, Robyn."

"What pregnancy test? Is that what he told you? I never thought I was pregnant. What a damn liar!"

"Oh?"

"That has nothing to do with why I called, Maggie. I'm not responsible for anything that man says. I called because I'd like to make up in some small way for my part in all this. You were a wonderful friend to me. I hate that we," she hesitated, "that *I* hurt you the way I did. I know I can't change what happened last summer, but I think I should let you know what he's up to now. Last week, Michael hired a private investigator to watch you. I feel sure he's down there now."

An icy chill ran through Maggie. "Why? Why on earth would he do that after the way he's treated our relationship?"

"Because he wants you back. I believe you'll know why if you give it a little thought. Mine obviously wasn't enough. And you should know Michael well enough to realize that he can't, or won't, accept 'no' for an answer when he wants a yes! Goodbye, Maggie, and I'm sorry. If I could change it all, I would. Us, I mean. I'm truly sorry for my part, but someday I think you'll thank me."

"Wait, Robyn..." She heard the click as Robyn hung up.

"Your *what* wasn't enough? Enough what?" She asked of no one.

As Maggie put the receiver back on its cradle, the scene of the stranger shaking hands with Kevin in the churchyard flashed into her mind's eye.

Chapter Fifteen

Maggie's mind spun. *Lil. I've got to go talk to Lil*, she thought. She tried to call Ross before leaving, but all she reached was his answering machine. "I'll call him again when I get back from Lil's," she said aloud, as she grabbed her jacket and purse and headed for the door.

When she reached her car, she looked around to see if anyone was watching. She saw nothing suspicious though it was dark and hard to spot anyone. She got into her car and drove the short distance to Lil's. When she pulled up in front of Lil's house, she was relieved to see that Kevin's car wasn't there. She would have gone back home had he still been at Lil's. She didn't want to talk to him; she wanted to explain the situation to Lil and have her talk with Kevin.

She looked about before getting out of the car. *What an awful way to have to live*, she thought. When she reached Lil's door, she made one more visual sweep of the neighborhood before ringing the bell. When she heard Lil's footsteps approaching the door, she called out, "It's Maggie."

A moment later, Lil opened the door smiling. "Maggie, come on in. I'm glad you came." She took one look into Maggie's eyes. "What's wrong? You look upset. What is it?"

"Oh Lil, I am. I have to talk to you. I should have confided in you sooner; if I had maybe things would be different now." Maggie sank down onto Lil's overstuffed sofa and inhaled deeply. Lil sat down beside her.

"For land's sake, tell me before I bust of curiosity." She turned to face Maggie as she waited for her to begin.

Maggie quietly recounted the details of her pregnancy to a speechless Lil. When she had finished Maggie looked at her friend. She couldn't suppress a little chuckle, "Lil, this is the first time since I've met you that I've seen you at a loss for words."

"I'm just tryin' to digest all of this, Maggie."

"I know, I'm dumping a lot on you all at once," Maggie said. Then she went on to tell Lil of Ross's and her feelings for one another.

Lil grinned her approval at that. "I'm happy the two of you finally realized you belong together, Maggie, but I gotta ask you something. Did you tell Kevin?"

"Only about Ross and me realizing we care for one another. And that's another thing I have to talk to you about, Lil. But what made you ask?"

"Somethin' about the way he acted after you and he talked this morning. It was his whole mood. Not so much anything he said; just his general attitude. And that stranger he was talkin' to after church. I asked him who he was, and Kev as much as told me it was none of my business. He said it was just a friend, but he didn't introduce me, and he didn't act like himself all afternoon. He was distracted. I might as well have been having lunch all by myself."

"Lil, I'm fearful that the stranger was the private detective that Michael hired to watch me, to find out what I'm doing and I'm not exactly sure what else. But it makes me feel terribly uneasy and frightened. I want Michael completely out of my life! I'm apprehensive, because I don't know what he's planning or what he's capable of doing. I used to think I knew Michael. Now, I realize how wrong I was. I *never* really knew him at all."

Lil drew in her breath. "Wow! This is serious. I gotta find out who that fellow was and see what Kevin told him."

"Thanks. You're a good friend. I knew I could count on you."

Lil stood and walked over to her phone. "I'm gonna call Kev and ask him to come to Serenity."

"Lil, I don't want to see or talk to him. I want you to handle this."

"I understand, Maggie. That's what I plan to do." She dialed Kevin's number and waited. After several rings he answered. "Kevin, it's me, Aunt Lil." She listened for a moment. "It's really important that I talk to you tonight. That'll be fine. Thanks, Kev. I'll be waiting." She put the receiver down and turned to Maggie. "He was on a business call, but he said he'll call me back as soon as they hang up."

"Good." Maggie breathed a sigh of relief. "I think I'll go on home. Will you please call me after you talk to him?"

"I sure will, honey. But what I'm thinking of doing is asking him if he can come down tomorrow or meet me halfway, so we can talk in person. I hate to go into all this on the phone. So, I may not have much to tell you."

"That's probably a good idea. Do you think he'll be able to get away so early in the week?"

"From what he tells me, he kind of sets his own schedule. I'll tell him it's really important to me. I think he'll make time for me. At any rate, I'll call you after we talk tonight."

"Thanks, Lil." Maggie gave her a quick hug and left.

...

When she reached her apartment she sank onto her sofa. "Why does everything have to be so complicated?" she asked aloud.

She phoned Ross to say goodnight. She had decided not to say anything to him about the call from Robyn and her discussion with Lil until she heard back from Lil. There was nothing Ross could do about it, and she knew it would anger him. No sense in them both being upset, and, besides, she hadn't seen anything suspicious this evening. What if Robyn had made the whole thing up? Still, the thought of the stranger, coupled with Robyn's call, did add credibility to her story. But, why? There wasn't a single scenario that she could come up with that would justify Michael's reasoning for hiring a private detective to spy on her.

She went into the bedroom and had just slipped into her nightgown when she heard the phone ring. She hurried to answer it. It was Lil.

"Maggie, I just finished talkin' to Kev, and he said tomorrow was busy for him. But he said if I could come to Sanford midday, he'd come down and meet me for lunch."

"I'm so relieved. Do you think you can get away from the drugstore? And, by the way, Ross doesn't know about Robyn's call or you talking to Kevin. I knew it would upset him, and I wanted everything resolved before I told him about it."

"My lips are sealed. I know how to handle Ross, been doing it for years."

"Please, call me at work just as soon as you get back tomorrow."

"I'll do it."

They said goodnight. Maggie made herself a cup of tea before settling down for a restless night of sleep.

...

Monday, Maggie wore a white maternity smock to work. She had ordered it out of a J. C. Penney catalog a couple weeks earlier. To her surprise, no one made any comment, so she didn't either. Perhaps no one realized it was a maternity smock. She decided to let time make her condition clear to everyone, and from the weight she had gained recently she didn't think it would take long.

The busy morning schedule helped the time pass, but Maggie was aware that she was glancing at her watch between each patient, picturing Lil on her way, then meeting with Kevin, and wondering how long it would be before Lil returned and called her.

Sanford, NC 12:30 P.M.

Lil swung her navy-blue Chevy Corsica into the Kentucky Fried Chicken parking lot and turned off the ignition. She waited only a few minutes before Kevin pulled into the parking place beside her. They got out of their cars and went inside. After going through the buffet line, they found a seat at the rear of the dining room. For the height of the noon hour, there wasn't much of a crowd. Lil was glad. It afforded her more privacy for their discussion.

"I've got to admit you have my curiosity up, Aunt Lil. You call and say you have to talk to me right away, that it's urgently important, and that it's about Maggie."

"That's all true, Kev."

"Well, you know I'm interested in anything to do with Maggie. Have she and Ross had a falling out?"

"I know that, Kev. And, no. They're very much together. But why are you so interested in her?" Lil asked.

"Maggie's an interesting and lovely lady," Kevin replied.

"But, Kevin, you hardly know her. And now you know she's in love with someone else."

"Aunt Lil, are you so sure that's going to last?"

"I am. I've seen this happening to them for weeks. They're so alike. I'm sure this is for keeps, Kevin. And I also know she told you of her feelings for Ross yesterday."

"You're right, she did." His manner became abrupt. "Now tell me why you had to see me today?"

"Kevin, Maggie's former fiancé, a Dr. Michael Kerns has been trying to persuade Maggie to give him another chance. She doesn't want anymore to do with him. He did something inexcusable, she caught him in the act, and it was something Maggie isn't willing to give him a chance to do to her again. He was around town a while back to see her. Told her he and her former best friend were going to have a child and that he was going to marry the girl."

"That's some pretty tough stuff, Aunt Lil."

"And that's not the end of it. A few weeks later he called her and told her he wanted her back, that the girl wasn't really pregnant. Maggie said under no circumstances but he doesn't seem to have taken 'no' for an answer. Now there's something Maggie doesn't want him to know, and it's not going to be a secret around Serenity for long. Maggie's pregnant. And, she absolutely *does not* want Michael to know. So, if anyone comes around asking questions about her, and they might, I'm asking you not to tell them *anything* about Maggie. I'm telling you this because there was that stranger in Serenity yesterday. You and he were talkin'. Now, I know it probably has nothing to do with all this. But Maggie had a call last night, and the woman told her that Michael had hired a private investigator to follow her and report back to him. It's like he's obsessed with her. I don't like it, Kev. I don't like it at all!"

"Aunt Lil, stop! Don't tell me anything else. I know the man. Michael Kerns is a client of mine."

Chapter Sixteen

"Kevin! How could you?" Lil's face flushed scarlet, and her voice was angry. "You let me tell you everything there was to tell. You should have stopped me at the beginning. What on earth could you possibly be doing for this Dr. Kerns?"

"I'm not at liberty to say; that's attorney-client privilege."

"Quit! Tell him you can't represent him, that it's a conflict of interest!" she demanded. "I thought you liked Maggie."

"I can't." His voice was quiet but firm. "We have an agreement. I can't break it. That's all I can tell you, Aunt Lil."

"I don't know you, Kevin Williams! I don't know you at all. All this high-and-mighty law business. It's corrupted you! I thought you were that same sweet boy who left here because he felt he'd make things better for me, misguided as that was. But you're some stranger I don't even know anymore. You know that Maggie is special to me. You've put me smack-dab in the middle now, Kev. How could you do this to all of us?"

"I'm sorry, Aunt Lil. I know you don't understand but

this is my *business*. It's what I'm paid to do, plain and simple as that."

"You know, I don't think you were ever really interested in Maggie. I think you were…" She stopped and looked Kevin in the eye. "Just how long *have* you known Michael Kerns?"

Kevin's eyes met his aunt's but he made no reply.

…

Kevin tried to hug his aunt when they parted, but she pulled away from him and left abruptly. As she drove back to Serenity, Lil felt anything but serene. She was angry and slightly nauseated. She hated the prospect of telling Maggie what she had done; she had poured out Maggie's problems to the very person who now legally represented the source of her dilemma. How could her attempt to help Maggie have turned into such a fiasco? Why had Kevin let her tell him so much before he stopped her? She thought she knew the answer to that question!

And Kevin! Why would he take on a client who might wish to hurt Maggie? How long had he been acquainted with Michael Kerns? Why didn't Maggie know him if he knew Michael. Had he only feigned interest in the girl to gather information that could be used against her? What had made him reappear on the scene at precisely the time he had? Was Maggie the only reason he had come back to Serenity? Questions rolled over and over in Lil's mind as she drove until she became aware that she had entered the Serenity town limits.

She knew Maggie was eagerly awaiting her call, but how she dreaded what she had to tell her. She wondered for a moment if she should stop by the drugstore first and talk to Ross about it. Then she thought better of that idea. Maggie deserved to know first, and Ross was going to be furious with Kevin, probably with her too. There was no love lost between those two before, and now this! No. She would call Maggie and ask her to stop by her place after work. She glanced at her watch. It was only about forty minutes until quitting time, if today happened to be a slow day.

She stopped by the drugstore briefly and told Ross she wasn't feeling well. It was no lie. Her head felt as if it could split in two.

Ross took one look at her and said, "You don't look too good, Lil. You need to go on home and get some rest. Are you sure you feel like driving?"

She nodded wearily. "Thanks, Ross. I'll see you in the morning."

"I'll check on you later. If you aren't feeling a hundred percent, you stay home tomorrow, too."

"I'll be alright. I have one of my sick headaches," she told him.

"You're doing too much, Lil. Maybe you need to take a couple days off. Talk to you later."

She nodded. "Thanks, Ross. We'll see."

Lil drove the short distance to her place and went inside. She sat down in her easy chair and reached for the phone. She felt as if she had a hive of bees swarming in her stomach. She dialed Doc's office number. Mildred answered. Lil asked for Maggie and waited for her to come on the line. After what seemed an interminable wait, she heard Maggie's voice.

"Sorry to keep you waiting, but I was in the middle a suture removal. How did it go?"

"Well, there's too much to go into on the phone," she began.

"I've had you on my mind all afternoon." Maggie sounded so hopeful, so totally trusting that Lil had made everything right.

Lil tried to sound upbeat. "Maggie, can you come by the house on your way home, honey?"

"Sure, Lil. Shall I pick up some sandwiches for us on the way?"

"Not unless you want one. I'm not very hungry, but I have some left over pork roast and gravy. I can fix you a hot sandwich, if that suits you."

"Sounds great! I'll see you as soon as I can get away." Maggie put the receiver down feeling intensely eager to hear what Lil had to tell her.

The last patient left the office by ten past five, and Doc told Maggie that he and Kathryn would handle the clean up. Maggie decided to stop by her apartment briefly to pick up the coconut cake she had bought recently. It was too much of a temptation for her. She'd leave the half that was left at Lil's.

She unlocked the door, went into the kitchen and removed the cake from the refrigerator. She noticed on her answering machine that she had two messages. She had decided against having her number changed. She was through running away. She had found her home in Serenity, and she wasn't going to let Michael be the cause of her living in fear for the rest of her life. Ross had an extra answering machine that he had given her. He thought it would be a wise way for her to monitor her calls.

She stepped over to the machine and pressed the play button. "Maggie, its Aunt Em. An attorney from Alexandria called here for you. He said he was from…" There was a brief silence and Maggie could hear paper rustling. "Oh, here it is, dear. His firm is Whitton, White, and Weston. He said it was *imperative* that his firm contacts you. I gave them your number. I hope that was all right. Call me. Love you, dear. Bye, Maggie."

Maggie's stomach began to churn. "I don't need this," she said aloud as the second message began. "Miss Thornton, this is Calvin Whitton with the firm of Whitton, White, and Weston in Alexandria, Virginia. There is a matter of utmost importance that I need to discuss with you." He gave her his phone number and asked her to call him at once and set up an appointment to come to his office. She jotted the number down on a post-it note then dialed Ross.

His phone rang five times before his machine came on. "Ross, I need to talk to you," Maggie said. "I'm going over to Lil's for dinner, but I'll call when I 'm ready to leave, and I hope you can meet me here."

She picked up the cake, reached for her purse and headed for Lil's. As she drove she pondered the attorney's message. Perhaps Michael had hired them, but why? What could he possibly need a lawyer for? Well, if he had hired them—and she would call them in the morning to see what this was all about, perhaps she could hire Kevin to represent her. She parked in front of Lil's and got out of her car.

When Lil answered the door, Maggie was stunned. "Lil, what's wrong? You look awful."

"Oh, Maggie, come on in. I didn't want to tell you on the phone, but it didn't go well with Kevin. In fact, it was a disaster." Lil began to sob.

Maggie put her arms around Lil and remained silent until the older woman composed herself enough to talk.

"I went there to help you, and I only made matters worse," Lil said dejectedly. She relayed her conversation with Kevin to Maggie including some of the questions that had run through her mind during her drive back.

Maggie listened without comment until Lil was finished. "Well, that makes me even more curious about the message I had from an Alexandria legal firm. I know you were trying to help me. Don't blame yourself; I certainly don't. I'm beginning to think Michael is unbalanced; none of this makes sense to me."

"It doesn't to me, either, Maggie. No sense at all."

"Would you be too upset if I don't stay for dinner? I need to talk to Ross. He doesn't know any of this, I mean about the detective or anything. He doesn't know, does he?"

"Not from me. I did enough damage with Kevin."

"If you don't mind, I'll call him from here. It'll save

time. If he's in, he can meet me at my place."

"Sure, honey. And I'm so relieved that you aren't angry with me."

"Why would I be? You went there with the best of intentions at my request. You certainly had no way of knowing that Kevin had any connection with Michael."

She dialed Ross's number. He picked up on the second ring.

"I've been waiting for your call," he told her. "I'm on my way now. See you in about ten minutes."

"Be careful! And don't get a ticket. I have so much to tell you!" *I wonder how you're going to react when you hear this latest bit of information.*

Chapter Seventeen

Ross pulled into Maggie's driveway as she got out of her car. "I'll bet that's a new record."

He leaned down to kiss her. "Could be."

He followed her up the stairs. "What's on your mind? Your message sounded pretty urgent."

Maggie quickly relayed everything that had happened, from Robyn's call and Lil's meeting with Kevin, to the message from the attorney, which she replayed for Ross.

"That explains why Lil looked the way she did this afternoon. That son-of-a-bitch! I haven't liked, or trusted, him from the first time I met him."

"I know you haven't. I couldn't seem to either. I wanted to like him, for Lil's sake, but he's really let her down, too. She's terribly hurt and upset with him."

"I told her I'd call later to check on her, but I haven't yet. How did she seem when you left her?"

"I think she was relieved to get it off her chest. She felt just awful about telling Kevin about the baby. I reminded her that it would be an impossible secret to keep. She seemed a little better when I left than she was when I arrived."

"Maggie, do you want me to be here with you when you call that attorney tomorrow?"

"Yes, that would make it easier. I plan to try to reach him first thing. That reminds me, I need to call Doc and see if I can be a few minutes late in the morning."

As she expected, Doc was agreeable. Ross stayed for another hour. Before he left, he offered to spend the night if Maggie wanted him to.

"I promise to stay on the sofa," he said with a wink.

"Thanks, Ross. I'll be fine, really."

He looked a little disappointed, but he kissed her and left. Though she felt exhausted by the time she got into bed, she tossed and turned for more than two hours before falling asleep.

She was awake before seven the next morning. She rose and fixed breakfast then dressed for work. At eight forty-five, Ross arrived.

Maggie waited until five after nine to try to reach the attorney. A receptionist answered, "Whitton, White, and Weston. How may I direct your call?"

"My name is Margaret Thornton. I had a message from Calvin Whitton asking me to call him. Is he available?"

"One moment, please." Musak played in Maggie's ear. She waited a little nervously, unsure of what to expect.

"Miss Thornton?" The slightly, gravely voice of Calvin Whitton came on the line. "Thank you for returning my call. I've been trying for some time to locate you."

"Why?" Maggie asked.

"Haven't you spoken with your attorney?"

"My attorney?"

"Yes; Kevin Williams. He called several days ago on your behalf. Frankly, I had expected you to get in touch with me as soon as you spoke with him."

"Well...he hasn't contacted me. What did you tell him?" Maggie asked calmly trying to hide the shock and anger rising within her.

"That I really need to meet with you personally to take care of the legal paperwork and view the necessary documentation."

"For what?" Maggie felt bewildered. This conversation was like being on a runaway merry-go-round.

"I'm sorry, Miss Thornton. I thought you and your fiancé had discussed this."

"My fiancé?"

"Michael Kerns. Dr. Kerns is the one who finally gave me your aunt Emily's phone number. Perhaps I should start at the beginning."

"Please do, thank you."

"I'm sure you've been following the class-action law suit against Capital Airlines in the newspaper. The suit involves negligence on their part in the crash that killed your father and sister."

"No. I wasn't aware of that."

"Well, It's been in the papers around here for weeks now. A settlement was reached a short while ago. My firm is handling the disbursement of the funds. After I learned that your mother was deceased, I began trying to contact you. I called the hospital where you were formerly employed, and Dr. Kerns happened to be in the administrator's office at the time. I spoke with him, and he took my number. He called back with your aunt's phone number, said you were visiting there for a while. Your aunt seemed puzzled as to why he would say that, but she was kind enough to give me a number for you. Now, when can you meet with me here at my office?"

Maggie was silent.

"I'll need death certificates for your father, sister and mother." He hesitated. "Miss Thornton, did you hear me?"

"Uh, yes. Yes, I heard you. I'll have to make arrangements; you've taken me by surprise."

"You do have the death certificates, don't you?"

"I have my mother's, and I have a metal box of papers she kept. I would imagine my father and sister's certificates are in there, but I'll have to check. May I call you back?"

"That will be fine. I'll be in the office until around one this afternoon. Miss Thornton, aren't you even curious about the sum of money you'll be receiving?"

"Oh, I...I guess so," Maggie answered haltingly.

"I must say your fiancé was more curious than you seem to be."

"Did you tell him?" Maggie asked.

"No. I didn't, but there has been a good deal about it in the news, and the figures of the settlement are a matter of public record now. Miss Thornton, between the flight insurance your father had on himself and your sister and the settlement of the suit, you'll be receiving roughly two million dollars."

Maggie's breath caught in her throat.

"Miss Thornton, are you all right?"

"Yes. I'm just totally shocked! Thank you, Mr. Whitton. I'll go through my papers and call you back."

Maggie hung up and looked at Ross. "You aren't going to believe this!"

Ross raised his eyebrows. "What now, Maggie? Good news or bad?"

"I guess it's mixed. Mr. Whitton said there has been a class action lawsuit against the airline, for negligence, in the crash that killed my father and sister. It's just been settled. He's holding a large amount of money for me. He's talked to Michael; that's how he got my aunt's number. He said Michael was very curious, and evidently led Mr. Whitton to believe that he's still my fiancé. Then Kevin Williams called him, representing himself as my attorney, to find out the details."

"Huh!" Ross shook his head. "Things are beginning to make a little more sense. The web of mystery starts to unravel.

That little piece of information Mr. Whitton gave you may be just what we need to take care of Kevin Williams. His actions are totally unethical."

"Do you think we could ask Mr. Whitton to document his statement that Kevin represented himself as my attorney?"

"I don't see why not. Kevin's way out of line."

"Ross, do you think it really was Kevin, or do you think Michael might have called and represented himself as Kevin?"

"I don't know. But, I intend to find out."

"I'll see what Mr. Whitton says when I call him back. I just don't understand why Michael is so interested in my money. I know he makes a hefty salary at the hospital. But, it certainly sounds as if he's trying to get me back for the money."

"Remember, it's not what you make but, how you handle it."

"You're right about that." Maggie went into her bedroom and removed her mother's metal box from its storage place in her closet. She carried it to her bed and sat down.

As she opened it, melancholy swept through her. Her eyes moistened. She had carried it with her but had been unable to open it before today. The time hadn't been right. She'd been too close to losing them. It was as if not inspecting the contents of the box had somehow allowed her to avoid the finality of it all. This little container that held the important records of their lives was all that was tangible of the family she loved so dearly.

Carefully, she sorted through the papers. There were birth certificates, her parent's marriage license, a copy of the deed for the house that had been sold to help pay her mother's medical expenses, some old bank registers and the death certificates for her father and sister. She removed her mother's death certificate from an envelope in her dresser drawer. She walked back to her bed and sat in silence, pressing the forms to her breast for a few moments, inhaling deeply as if she could catch the scent of them, breathe their essence into her. She felt close to them and overwhelmingly sad for the loss of them. Minutes later, she wiped her eyes and went back into the living room.

"I've found them, Ross," she said softly. She lifted the receiver and dialed Mr. Whitton's office. She waited only a moment before he answered. Maggie told him she had found what he needed, then listened.

When he finished speaking, she asked, "Will you please hold for a minute?" She covered the speaker portion of the phone. "Ross, he wants to know if I can meet with him this Friday at two o'clock. Will you go with me?"

"You know I will. Let's talk to him in person about Kevin though. What do you think?"

"I agree."

She returned to Mr. Whitton. "That sounds fine. I'll plan to see you then."

"Will your lawyer accompany you, Miss Thornton?"

"No, I'll be with my fiancé." She noticed, out of the corner of her eye, that Ross was smiling.

The arrangements having been completed, Mr. Whitton put his secretary on the line to give Maggie directions.

Friday 1:30 P.M.

Ross parked on the third level of the high rise parking deck across the street from the law firm of Whitton, White and Weston in one of their allotted spaces.

Since he and Maggie had arrived a little early, as planned, they sat in the car and talked for a few minutes before going over to the appointment.

Once inside, they looked at the building directory then waited for the elevator. Ross leaned down and whispered, "Impressive. They have the entire top three floors of this four story building."

Maggie nodded in agreement. She had butterflies in

her stomach, and she wasn't sure why. She and Ross were the only ones on the elevator. When it stopped on the fourth floor, they got out and checked the directory.

Once in Mr. Whitton's waiting room, it took only a few minutes before the secretary told them the attorney was ready to see them. They stepped over to the door; the secretary opened it and motioned for them to go in.

Maggie looked about the impressive décor. The office was large, octagonal and quite elegantly furnished. Mr. Whitton was seated, at his mahogany desk, in a muted burgundy and navy striped velveteen chair that had gold upholstery studs decorating each arm. She noticed that the client chairs were done in solid burgundy and navy. The colors were arranged intermittently in a semi-circle facing the front of Mr. Whitton's desk. At the far end of the room was an octagonal mahogany conference table surrounded by eight chairs that matched the client chairs in front of his desk. Mahogany bookcases, with beautifully bound leather books, lined the entire room and only broke for the double doors that admitted Maggie and Ross into his inner-sanctum.

Mr. Whitton rose from his chair as they stepped into the room. He was a big man, over six feet tall and, though his frame was large, he looked fit. He wore a three-piece, gray, pinstripe suite and a stiffly starched white shirt. His hair must have been prematurely silver, as Maggie judged by his skin tone that he was no more than fifty, if that. To her, he looked the epitome of a big city corporate lawyer.

"Miss Thornton, a pleasure to meet you," he said, as he motioned toward the chairs in front of him. "Please, have a seat."

Maggie walked across the thick plush navy carpet until she stood directly in front of his desk. Before she could introduce Ross, Mr. Whitton spoke again.

"Well, Dr. Kerns. At last we meet in person." He extended his right hand across his desk to Ross.

Ross took his hand. "I'm Ross Harrington, Mr. Whitton. I'm Maggie's fiancé."

Mr. Whitton gave Maggie a puzzled look. "But I thought you said Michael Kerns was your fiancé." He quickly glanced at the folder that lay open before him.

Maggie looked at Ross. "No, that's what Michael told you. Michael and I haven't been engaged for several months."

"Hmmm, then at the time I spoke with the hospital administrator, you and Dr. Kerns were no longer planning to be married. Is that correct?"

"That's correct."

Calvin Whitton glanced down at the open folder again. "And this attorney Kevin Williams. Is he, in fact, your legal counselor?"

"No, he isn't. And, I want to talk to you about his call," Maggie said.

Ross had taken a chair to her right, but he remained silent. He wouldn't involve himself in the discussion unless Maggie needed him to.

"I see, Miss Thornton. Go ahead, please."

"I'd like to have a statement in writing from you that a man representing himself as my attorney and calling himself Kevin Williams contacted you on my behalf about this settlement." Maggie sounded very controlled.

"Might I ask why, Miss Thornton?"

Maggie looked at Ross. He gave her hand a little squeeze.

"Mr. Whitton, I'd rather not go into detail. This in no way involves you. But I would like your verification, if you'll give it to me." She spoke quietly and looked him in the eye.

"Well, I would hope you don't blame me for speaking to Mr. Williams. I speak with clients' attorneys quite regularly. It's very common, you know"

"I understand that. And in no way do I wish to involve you in my situation with Mr. Williams, except that I need your statement."

Mr. Whitton looked quite solemn. "You do involve me, or I should say that I involve myself by giving you my statement, Miss Thornton."

Maggie met his gaze in silence.

Abruptly, Calvin Whitton smiled at Maggie. "I'll give you what you ask for. You're a no-nonsense lady. I *like* that. If I need to become involved, if someone is trying to unethically maneuver you into something, I'm not quite sure what this is all about, you call on me, and I'll set the record straight."

"Thank you." For the first time since their discussion began, Maggie smiled, too.

By the time she and Ross left the law office, she had given Mr. Whitton copies of the three death certificates and had signed all the legal insurance and court documents necessary. She also carried with her the all important letter stating that Kevin had called Mr. Whitton representing himself as Maggie's attorney, written on Whitton White and Weston's letterhead and signed by Calvin Whitton.

Mr. Whitton had told her that it should take about a week for the financial matters to be finalized. He had given her the option of having the funds deposited directly into her bank account or having a check from the firm's escrow account sent directly to her. She had conferred with Ross on that matter. After discussion, Maggie told Mr. Whitton to send the check to her personally. This would give her a little more time to decide exactly how to handle this matter. She didn't want any information of this newfound wealth leaking out around Serenity. News had a way of spreading in a small town, and Maggie wanted to avoid that if at all possible.

...

Once they were back in Ross's car, Maggie said, "I appreciate the way you let me handle that meeting, Ross. I couldn't help but think that if I'd been with Michael, he'd have stepped in right at the start and tried to do all the talking."

"You didn't need me to say anything, Maggie. You handled Mr. Whitton as one lawyer to another. Perhaps you missed your calling," he chuckled.

Maggie looked at him. "Oh, I don't know about that, but thanks, I'm grateful. I really mean it."

Maggie looked at her watch. It was nearly four o'clock and traffic was beginning to become very congested in downtown Alexandria. "I think we'd better find a motel and go back in the morning, Ross. Suddenly I feel very tired. I guess that meeting was more wearing on me than I realized at the time."

"You're sure, Maggie?" he asked.

They had packed overnight bags just in case.

"I'm sure, Ross," she said softly. "I'm very sure."

Chapter Eighteen

Forty minutes later, Ross parked beneath the sheltered overhang at a Ramada Inn on the south side of Alexandria. "You wait here while I go in and register." He set the emergency brake and turned off the ignition.

"Let me go. I want to pay for our room."

"Did I hear you say 'room,' singular?" He asked with a grin spreading across his face. "And no, I won't hear of it. You paying, I mean. Not the single room. Never let it be said that Ross Harrington is, or ever has been, a kept man."

"You took the day off for me. It shouldn't cost you."

"Believe me, I didn't do it just for you. I did it for us, and I'd have worried to think of you alone on the highway for such a long trip."

"I made the trip to Serenity alone and did just fine," she reminded him.

"That was then, before I knew you and loved you and before you were pregnant." He caught the look in her eye. "All right. Two out of three. Anyway, I'm paying for the room, and that's that. You wait here. I'll register us and come back for you and our bags."

"I give up," she laughed, raising her arms skyward.

When Ross returned, he brought a luggage carrier with him. He popped the trunk and loaded their bags onto it. Maggie waited at the front door with their belongings, while Ross found a parking place.

He joined her moments later. "We're lucky we weren't any later. The man who registered right after I did got the last vacancy. As luck would have it, I had to take a king size bed."

"I hope they have a comfortable chair for you to sleep in," she countered and winked at him.

"You're a hard-hearted little woman, Maggie Thornton."

They rode the elevator to the second floor. They found their room at the far end of the hall. It looked to have been newly renovated and was very tastefully appointed. In addition to the bed, they had two easy chairs and a table, a desk and a compact refrigerator.

"Very nice. And look, Ross," she said, pointing toward the corner of the room." You should be real comfortable if you pull that chair up to face the other one."

He looked at her quite solemnly, "You're serious, aren't you?"

She walked over to him, wrapped her arms around his neck and brushed the corner of his mouth with her tongue ever so lightly. Then, she leaned into him and gave him a lingering kiss. "What do you think?" she whispered against his lips.

He pulled her even more tightly against him and answered with another kiss.

"You'd better stop that," he whispered into her ear, "or I just might not let you leave the room for dinner."

"Don't forget. I'm eating for two, now."

"What are you in the mood for? The desk clerk said there are several good restaurants close by."

"Any place is fine with me. You choose," she told him.

She stepped out of his embrace and went into the bathroom to freshen up.

…

He chose a seafood restaurant, and they weren't disappointed. Maggie's broiled scallops were done to perfection, and Ross found the seafood variety platter he ordered equally enjoyable. Neither could finish everything on their plates.

"Let's get a takeout box," Maggie suggested. "I don't have the heart to waste such delicious food, and we do have a fridge in our room."

"You know we'll probably throw it out in the morning," Ross said. "But, I agree, it is too good to give up on just yet."

…

It was nearly ten when they got back to their room. Maggie told Ross to go ahead and take his shower first. She had noticed an iron in the closet and wanted to press an outfit for tomorrow.

To her surprise, she began to feel a little ill at ease with this man she had always been so comfortable with. At first, she chalked it up to fatigue, then she had to admit that, for as much as she wanted Ross to make love to her, she knew he had been so in love with Melanie. She had to acknowledge that she feared he might compare her to his ex-wife. Perhaps she would come up short. What if she disappointed him? After all, she no longer had the figure she had when first she met him. On this, their first time, how would he feel about that? She could feel the butterflies beginning to stir in her stomach.

Ross stepped out of the bathroom wearing a forest green terry cloth robe, his hair still damp but neatly combed, and Maggie's heart rate accelerated at the sight of him.

"Next," he said, smiling as he motioned her toward the bathroom. "I'll be waiting." He pulled her tightly to him and kissed her.

The fresh, clean scent of him sent a thrill through her. She pressed her face against his chest through the opening in his robe and caressed it with her lips.

Moments later, when he released her, with a whispered, "Hurry," she gathered her sleepwear from her suitcase and disappeared into the bathroom.

She couldn't erase the sight and feel of him from her mind as she stood in the shower with the soothing, warm water washing over her, relaxing her and calming the butterflies. He had marvelous legs, firm and muscular. His shoulders were so broad, his waist so trim, and she found the way his robe lay open two thirds of the way down his chest so very sensual. She could feel herself becoming even more aroused.

Ten minutes later she emerged from the bathroom wearing a soft yellow cotton batiste full length nightgown with an empire waistline and spaghetti straps that accentuated her full breasts. Ross drew in his breath as he gazed at her.

"You're so beautiful." His voice had a husky quality.

She stepped into his embrace. His hands caressed her body, intensifying her desire for him. She stroked his chest softly for a moment as she kissed him. Then her hands moved downward and loosened the belt on his robe. Her fingers traced a path to his collarbone and she slid his robe off of his shoulders. He released her just long enough to let it fall to the floor. Then he reached for the straps of her gown and pushed them down off of her shoulders. He kissed her eyelids, her lips, her cheek, then her neck and finally his lips found her breasts. Then, he swept her into his arms, carried her to the edge of the bed and gently laid her down. Still kissing her, he lowered himself over her. Maggie was lost in the pleasure of this moment and the man she loved. She no longer had any self-doubts.

...

She had fallen asleep in his arms. She awakened a couple hours later to go to the bathroom. One of the curses of pregnancy, she called it. After she returned to their bed, she had relived their earlier moments of love making before drifting back to sleep. She had found Ross a wonderful lover. He was so tender and patient making sure to take plenty of time with her to insure her satisfaction. Maggie appreciated this all the more, because she knew it had been a long time for him. He had been highly aroused from the beginning, but she had still been his main concern. How could Melanie have ever walked away from that kind of love? And then, all Maggie could think of, was that she would be forever grateful to her for doing so. This had been the most wonderful night of Maggie's life.

Within moments, she drifted into sleep with a faint smile on her lips. His handsome face was the first sight to greet Maggie's eyes when she awakened the next morning.

They slept fairly late for both of them. Ross made coffee in their room, and Maggie read several articles aloud from the complimentary *USA Today* that was left outside their door.

"You know, this is like being married, getting up late on a Saturday morning and having coffee while we read the paper together. At least the way I picture marriage," he added, "feels good to me."

"It is good," Maggie agreed. "And so comfortable." She looked at him with his hair tussled from sleep and wearing the green robe she found so sensuous. But what gave her the most satisfaction was how happy he seemed these days. She couldn't suppress her pleasure.

"What are you smiling about?" He asked her, running his hands through his hair to smooth it back.

"Just you, Ross. I'm smiling at you because I love you, and I feel like the luckiest person on earth."

He smiled at her for a moment then rose from his chair

at the table, walked around to her seat and gently pulled her to her feet. He kissed her tenderly then whispered into her ear, "How can you be when I am?"

...

It was after one before they left the motel and headed for North Carolina.

Traffic was lighter as it was a Saturday, and they were able to make good time. When they reached the Raleigh area it was still light.

"I'd like to stop at a phone booth and look up the address of the law firm Kevin Williams works for. Is that all right with you, Maggie?"

"Why?"

"Well, I've been thinking. Since we have that letter from Calvin Whitton, I'd like to make a copy of it and confront Kevin with it. Who knows what I may find out that way."

"I hadn't thought of that. Perhaps it would prove interesting. But, would you rather I did it, maybe the next time he comes to town?"

"Absolutely not. I don't trust that bastard. I don't want you around him. No, I plan to meet him on his own turf. I'll come up to see him the first of the week."

They found a phone book, looked up the address, and rode by. It was a large impressive building of glass and stone. There was an immense, man-made pond with a fountain to the side of the building. Flower gardens with a picnic area surrounded the pond on three sides.

"Not bad working conditions, wouldn't you say?"

"Not bad, is right," she agreed.

When they arrived in Serenity it was nearly seven o'clock. "Let's stop by my place and fix something to eat, Maggie. I'm not ready to give you up yet."

...

Ross put a couple steaks on the grill while Maggie fixed a tossed salad.

She had set the kitchen table, poured him a glass of wine and had the candles lit when he came in from the deck with the steaks.

"Now that's what I call a perfect ending to a perfect day. Well not quite the perfect ending but a prequel to it." He leaned down and kissed her.

"I hear you." She smiled at him as she wrapped her arms around his neck.

...

It was midnight when they left his place and drove back to town. "I'd like to keep you with me tonight. No one would know whether we were back or not."

"Oh, yes, they would, Ross. You know this town has eyes everywhere."

"Maggie, let's set a date. Let's make it in the next couple weeks. This weekend has spoiled me. I don't want to be without you another day."

Chapter Nineteen

At nine-thirty the following Tuesday, Ross left his home and headed for Raleigh. He carried along a copy of the letter Mr. Whitton had given Maggie. Before leaving, he called Kevin's office to make sure that he would be in that day. He hadn't tried to make an appointment; he didn't want to give Kevin the opportunity to turn him down. He'd take his chances just showing up.

A little over an hour later he stepped onto the elevator in Kevin's office building and pressed the third-floor button. He found the office Kevin shared with one other attorney, rechecked the breast pocket of his suit for the letter, opened the door and stepped inside.

The plump, graying receptionist was talking on the phone, so Ross took an empty seat and waited. There was one other man sitting in the waiting area.

When the woman hung the receiver up, she addressed the man who had been there when Ross arrived.

"Who are you here to see, sir?"

"I have an appointment with George Stillwell. I may be a few minutes early," he said.

She buzzed Mr. Stillwell then turned back to the man. "You can go on in now," she told him.

"And you, sir. Do you have an appointment?"

"I'm here to see Kevin Williams," Ross said matter-of-factly.

She glanced at a book that Ross assumed was an appointment book. "What is your name?" she asked.

"Ross Harrington."

"I don't see you scheduled in for today."

"Would you please ask Mr. Williams if he'll be kind enough to see me for a few minutes?"

She buzzed Kevin's office. "There's a gentleman here to see you." And, then to Ross, "I'm sorry, what did you say your name was, sir?"

"Harrington. Ross Harrington."

She repeated the name to Kevin then listened for a moment. "Certainly." She turned to Ross. "Mr. Williams is tied up for the entire day and won't be able to see you, Mr. Harrington. He asked me to give you his regrets."

Ross looked at the receptionist for a moment before rising and walking through the door of Kevin's office. She rose immediately and started after him.

"Sir, you can't go in there." Her voice was shrill, nervous. She was at Ross's heels as he stepped inside Kevin's office. "Sir! Please."

On seeing Ross, Kevin jumped to his feet and dropped the paperback he had been reading.

"You don't look so busy to me, Kevin."

Kevin's face paled. "What the hell do you want with me, Harrington?"

The receptionist gasped. "Sir," she asked in a high pitched voice, "shall I call security?"

"I wouldn't advise that, Kevin," Ross said calmly. "I

met with Calvin Whitton on Friday, and I have a letter with me that I think you'll find very interesting."

Kevin looked Ross in the eye then nodded at his secretary. "It's all right, Madeline. I'll see Mr. Harrington. I'll buzz you if I need anything."

The woman looked relieved. "Certainly, Mr. Williams." Then, looking sternly at Ross, she found her normal voice, "I'll be right outside."

Ross found it amusing. For an instant, he pictured the woman with a baseball bat awaiting Kevin's cry for help.

When they were alone, Kevin said, "Now, Harrington, sit down, and tell me what this is all about."

Ross and Kevin were sequestered behind the office door for more than an hour before Ross left. Once on the road again, he glanced at his watch. No wonder he felt hungry. He decided to stop at a Cracker Barrel restaurant before heading back to Serenity. He took his cell phone in with him, and, while he was eating, it rang. It was Lil.

"I'm sorry to interrupt you, Ross. But all of a sudden we have a slew of prescriptions coming in. I just wondered when you'd be back, 'cause you have several hours work here. I'll stay late and help you if you need me. I can start filling them but I can't dispense them without you here."

"Just wait for me. Thanks, Lil. I'm on my way."

...

Ross parked behind the drugstore, hurried inside and traded his suit jacket for a lab coat. Lil was busy in the pharmacy unpacking a shipment.

"You made it back in good time. Where'd you go, Ross, or is it a secret?" she asked with a grin.

"It's a secret for now, little lady." He winked at her.

"Okay, be that way." She was still smiling, but Ross could tell she was really curious.

"Now," he said, sorting through the pile of prescriptions on his spindle, "what's with all this? There wasn't a one when I checked with you mid-morning."

"It's the flu," Lil said. "We've had one after another either called in or brought by personally. I told everyone I'd phone them when they were ready for pick up."

"Then let's get busy," he said reaching for a large container of cough syrup. "Before I get started, I need to make a call." He put the bottle down, stepped to his phone and dialed a number.

"Is Maggie available?" He waited.

"Hi," he said. "I wanted you to know I'm back, and, I guess you already know this, we're snowed under here. I'll probably be a lot later than Lil tonight. I'll send her home after we notify folks that their medications are ready, but I'll stay on and dispense them and any advice necessary to go with them. There are a couple here that I'll have to deliver myself. All that aside, it went pretty well today," he continued in hushed tones. "I'll be surprised if we have any more problems from Kevin. Let's meet at the sandwich shop for lunch tomorrow, and I'll fill you in on everything."

Lil stepped up to him. "Ross, if that's Maggie, don't hang up, I want to talk to her."

"Honey, I'm going to turn you over to Lil now. I love you, bye."

Lil took the receiver from Ross and pressed it to her ear. "Hi, Maggie."

...

Ross began filling the first prescription. Lil joined him a few minutes later. Between them, they had most of them ready for pick up in a little over an hour. Lil began calling the patients. Between calls, the pharmacy phone rang.

"I've got half a mind to let that ring," Lil mumbled.

"Now, Lil, you know better. We can't do that."

"R.H. Pharmacy. How can we help you?" she said into the receiver. She looked a little puzzled. Not recognizing the voice she asked, "Who's calling?"

As she listened, her face paled. "You want to speak to Ross? Wait a minute." She removed the receiver from her ear and pressed it to her breast. "Ross," she said quietly.

He turned to face her. "My God, Lil what is it?"

Without a word she held the receiver out to him.

Chapter Twenty

"Hello?" Ross listened. He, too, looked shaken.

Lil tried to busy herself, but she was unable to force herself to concentrate on anything other than Ross's conversation. She could only make out a word here and there, as he spoke so softly it was barely discernible.

"Call me after ten at the house," she heard him say. "We'll discuss it then. Do you have the number?"

After he hung the phone up he seemed very agitated. "Lil, finish up the calls," he told her abruptly. Then you can leave. And please, don't mention this to *anyone*, and that means Maggie, too. I'll handle it. Do you understand? I may not be in until tomorrow afternoon."

"Okay, Ross. Whatever you say."

She finished her calls, put on her coat and hat and said goodnight, leaving the front door unlocked for their customers.

As she drove home, she mumbled to herself. "Dear, Lord, what next?" she kept asking. "What next?" As she pulled up to the front of her house and turned into the driveway, she noticed that Maggie had already arrived. "Oh, dear Lord," she said again.

Maggie was waiting on the front porch as Lil closed the garage door and came around to the front of the house. "Hi. I knew you'd be late, so, I picked up a chicken and some fixin's from the deli at the market. Since it's a new addition, I thought we should give them a try."

"That's thoughtful of you, honey. Thanks"

"You look beat, Lil. You sit down on the sofa and put your feet up, I'll have this on the table for us in no time. Or," she added as an afterthought, "we can eat off of TV tables, if you'd rather." She carried the food into the kitchen and laid it on the counter then rejoined Lil.

"Let's do that, but Maggie, you must be awful tired too." Lil kicked her shoes off and propped her legs up on the sofa.

"Oh, Lil, I feel so good these days. I can't believe it." Maggie sat at the opposite end of the sofa and began to massage the older woman's feet. "You know when all this happened with Michael, and then I realized I was pregnant, I felt as if I'd never smile again. And I definitely thought I'd never trust a man again, let alone fall in love. Then, Ross came into my life as a friend and confidant. He was so wonderful, so thoughtful, and he knew just what I'd been through. Day after day, I was falling so deeply in love with him. And the funny thing is, it was so natural and so gradual, that I really didn't see it coming. I think it happened the same way for him. Suddenly that night that I went out to his place for dinner, it just hit us both right between the eyes." Maggie laughed. "Listen to me rattling on and you so tired, Lil."

"Maggie, Honey," Lil's eyes teared. "How I hope this all works out for you. I wouldn't want you to get hurt again."

"Don't worry, Lil. I know exactly what I'm doing now. Everything about it feels right."

...

Wednesday morning

Midway through the morning Maggie received a phone call. Mildred buzzed her in the examining room. She picked up, said hello and listened.

"Well, good morning yourself," she responded, a flirtatious tone in her voice.

"Maggie, I have to cancel our lunch. Something urgent has come up. I have to attend to it today."

"What is it Ross? You sound so serious."

"I can't go into it now. I'll get back to you just as quickly as I can."

"Okay, call me as soon as possible. I love you," she added.

"I will, Maggie." He broke the connection.

Strange, Maggie thought, *he didn't seem himself at all.* She was curious all morning. At 12:30, they closed the office for lunch. It was the first day this week they had been able to do so. Doc, Katherine and Mildred were going home for lunch and invited Maggie to join them.

"Thanks, but I think I'll just run down the street and grab a sandwich at As You Like It," she told them. Besides, she thought the walk would do her good.

Five minutes later, she stepped inside the little lunch shop. Carl Warner greeted her.

"Hello, Maggie. How are you today?"

Maggie thought his voice sounded strained. He didn't look directly at her. Perhaps he was tired.

"We're kind a busy this noon. I doubt you'll want to wait. Can we fix you something for take-out? You can sit right here at the counter, and we'll have it ready in no time."

"That's all right, Carl. I don't mind a little wait," she

said walking toward the sitting area. "Maybe there's someone I know in there who wouldn't mind having me join them."

"But, Maggie," he said trying to step in front of her.

He was too late. Maggie stopped dead in her tracks and stared straight at the corner table at the far end of the room. The table she and Ross had shared the first time they had lunch together.

Ross was seated at the table, and Maggie could see the profile of a blond woman. They looked quite intent on one another as they spoke. The woman was very beautiful and quite tastefully dressed. The brown suit she wore had a leopard skin collar and cuffs; it looked expensive. As Maggie watched them in stunned silence, the woman reached across the table and laid her hand on Ross's forearm. Her nails were manicured and polished a deep plum hue. Ross leaned toward her. He made no move to withdraw from her touch.

Maggie gasped. Carl put his arm around her to steady her. She turned to look at Carl. "You know her, don't you? Tell me who she is, Carl." Her voice was barely audible.

"That's Melanie Harrington," he said softly.

His words confirmed what her heart and mind already knew.

Chapter Twenty-One

Somehow, Maggie had managed to retain her dignity and leave the sandwich shop without Ross seeing her. She returned to the clinic. She had to use her key to let herself in, as the others hadn't returned from lunch. She made it back to the break room before dissolving into tears.

Why? She wondered. Why was this happening to her all over again? *Why has Melanie chosen now to come back into Ross's life? What does she want from him? That looked apparent enough at lunch. And Ross, he wasn't smiling. His expression was serious, and he allowed her hand to remain on his arm.*

Maggie knew how deeply Ross had loved Melanie. Everyone in town knew it. If Melanie no longer meant anything to him, why hadn't Ross just told her, "Melanie's back and wants to talk to me. I'll have lunch with her to see what's on her mind. But it's you I love, Maggie. Don't worry. I'll see you tonight."

But he hadn't said that; he hadn't mentioned that the important matter he had to attend to was Melanie. *Why*? Why was he keeping this from her, and why were they there at the diner for everyone in town to see? Why had she let herself love him, opened herself up for another hurt?

She heard the door bang shut and voices in the hall. She took a Kleenex from her pocket and wiped her eyes. She blew her nose. Kathryn stepped into the break room.

"So, you beat us back, did you?" She smiled at Maggie. When Maggie looked up Katherine said, "Maggie! What's wrong?"

Maggie burst into tears again. Kathryn stepped into the hall and called Doc.

He came immediately, and seeing Maggie's condition, he nodded at his wife. "Go ahead, Dear, I'll be out directly." Kathryn Miller left them, closing the door behind her. "Now, Maggie, you calm yourself, and tell me what's wrong."

"Oh, Doc! Melanie's back in town," she blurted out through her tears. "And Ross cancelled with me to have lunch with her. He didn't tell me she was back. I just walked into the sandwich shop, and there they were. Carl tried to keep me from going in and finding them together."

"Here, here, child. You have to pull yourself together. Now I'm sure there's a perfectly logical explanation, and Ross will tell you when he sees you. Did you eat any lunch?"

"No. I was too upset."

"That isn't wise, is it?" he said in his calm, fatherly way.

"No," she agreed.

"Look at you, Maggie. Your face is all flushed and your pretty cheeks are streaked with tears. You can't be seeing our patients like that. I'm sending you home to rest this afternoon. But first, let's check your blood pressure." He reached for his stethoscope. He stuck his head out into the hall and asked for a cuff from one of the examining rooms.

When Kathryn brought it to him, he wrapped the cuff around her arm, pumped it up and listened. He repeated the procedure. His expression became grave.

"Can you give us a urine specimen?"

"I'll try. What's my blood pressure, Doc?"

"Too high, Maggie, way too high. 196 over 112."

"Oh my gosh!"

Maggie went into the hall, opened the supply cupboard and removed a specimen container. She went into the bathroom. Now she had yet another concern. "Please, God, let my baby be alright," she whispered.

When she came out, Doc met her in the hall. "You're going straight home, young lady. I've called Caroline. Charlie's on his way down to pick you up, and Caroline's making up the bed in their spare room for you. Leave your keys here. I'll drop your car off at the end of the day."

Maggie gave him no argument.

Charlie came in through the rear entrance five minutes later. Doc walked to the back door with them as they left.

"You call me if anything changes for the worse. Kathryn and I'll stop in when I leave your car off. Now, young lady, don't you worry about anything but getting some rest and staying calm. Like I said, I'm sure there's a logical explanation for what you saw earlier today. I don't think you have a thing to worry about when it comes to how Ross feels about you. Ross loves you. I've seen the look in his eyes when he's around you."

"I'll try, Doc. Thanks." Her eyes began to tear again.

Doc gave her arm a gentle pat. "You'll feel better with some rest," he said as he opened the back door of the clinic.

As soon as Charlie and Maggie were seated in the car, Charlie wanted to know what had happened.

"It's a long story. I'd rather tell you and Caroline at the same time, if you don't mind."

"I understand," he said sympathetically. They drove the short distance home in silence. Caroline stepped through the back door as soon as Charlie pulled into the driveway.

"Come on in, Maggie. I've put fresh linens on your bed

and have it turned back waiting for you. I'll run up and get one of your nightgowns and be back in a jiffy." Caroline told her.

"Thanks, but I'll go. I know right where everything is. I'll be right back."

Maggie let herself into her apartment and headed for her bedroom. As she passed the phone, it began to ring. *Perhaps it's Ross with an explanation,* she thought hopefully as she lifted the receiver and said hello.

She froze. Her pulse quickened as she recognized Michael's voice.

"Maggie, darling! I couldn't be happier. We'll be married right away. Our baby needs two parents. I knew we'd get back together. I love you."

"No!" She snapped. This is my child, not yours! You're not going to be part of my child's life."

Michael's tone changed from elation to surliness. "We'll see about that, you high and mighty…! If you don't marry me, I'll take you to court for custody of our child. When I'm through with you, you'll…."

Maggie slammed the receiver down, grabbed her nightgown from the closet and left her apartment in tears. Caroline met her at the door. Maggie fell into her arms, trembling and sobbing.

…

When Maggie was finally settled in bed, Caroline and Charlie sat in the bedroom with her as she relayed the events that had lead up to the reason for her temporary bed rest orders. Then she told them about Michael's call.

Charlie was furious. "Someone needs to get that man under control. If I ever catch sight of him around here, I'm just the one who'll do it!"

He's not your problem, Charlie. He's mine. I'll have to

deal with him myself. I was such a fool to ever become involved with him."

"You are our concern. And right now, you need something to eat and drink and some rest, Dear." Caroline embraced Maggie. "We could all use a little something." She went out to the kitchen and fixed a sandwich for Maggie and a cup of hot chocolate for all of them. She left Maggie's on the bedside table. She and Charlie took theirs out to the living room. Thirty minutes later when Caroline peered in at her, Maggie was sleeping soundly.

"Poor child," she said, rejoining Charlie. "She's had more than her share to deal with, hasn't she?"

"That she has, Caroline. That she has," he agreed.

"That horrid man, Michael. He worries me. And what on earth do you think has brought that *tramp* Melanie back to town?"

Charlie shook his head. "I wouldn't even hazard a guess as to how that woman thinks. I never did much like her even before she pulled what she did on Ross. She didn't fit in around here from the start. I never did see what he found so irresistible in her. I can't believe he'd be fool enough to take her back when a wonderful girl like Maggie loves him."

"Good Lord, Charlie! Surely you don't think he would, do you?"

"I wouldn't have thought he'd put up with her shenanigans for as long as he did. Remember that he was willing to forgive her. She was the one who wanted to end it."

"Well," Caroline continued, "there wasn't a wonderful girl like Maggie in the picture then, so let's hope and pray he has his wits about him now. He's such a smart man in every other way and such a good fellow."

"There's no sense sitting here hashing this over when we've got no control over any of it. You don't need to get yourself all upset, Caroline. That won't do you or Maggie any good. No, let's just be patient and see how it works itself out."

...

At two-thirty, Lil called Caroline. "I just talked to Doc, and he told me about Maggie. How is she?"

"She was mighty upset when Charlie brought her in, but she's sleeping right now."

"Poor Maggie. Elsie Hopkins stopped in a few minutes ago. She'd had lunch at the sandwich shop, and she couldn't wait to tell me that Ross was there having lunch with Melanie."

"I know, Lil. It's just awful."

"All I know is that Melanie called here at the drugstore last night," Lil began. "And, Ross seemed plenty upset when they hung up. He said he was going to deal with it and for me not to tell a soul and that meant Maggie, too. I felt just sick havin' dinner with her and her so happy and talkin about how she loves Ross and me not being able to say one word. I tell you, Caroline, if Ross takes *that woman* back after everything she pulled and hurts Maggie, I'll... I'll just.... I'm not sure what! I could just shake him for even agreeing to see her!"

"I know," Caroline sympathized.

"The minute he comes back to work, I'm gonna have a talk with him. You can bet your life on that! He tells *me* not to tell a soul, and then he has lunch with her down at Carl's, in broad daylight, where the whole town can see him. I just don't understand it. Uh oh, the other line's ringing, I gotta hang up."

The pharmacy 2:40 P.M..

It was Ross. "Lil, something has come up. I have to go somewhere, and I may not be back until tomorrow. I've arranged for a pharmacist friend of mine, from Sanford, to cover for me; he should be there any time now. Help him out, Lil. I'm counting on you."

"But Ross, Maggie…,"

He cut her off. "I'll talk to Maggie when I get back."

"But, Ross."

"Lil, I don't have time now," he snapped at her. "Bye." He hung up.

Lil slammed the receiver down. "Fine! You just go on about your business, Mr. Harrington! Don't say I didn't try to tell you."

She had never felt so angry with Ross as she did right now. He had never been so short with her before. *And what on earth is so pressing that he couldn't even let me tell him about Maggie?* She wondered. *Has he come under the spell of that Melanie all over again?* Lil shook her head. *I should have just hung up on her last night and told Ross it was a wrong number.* She knew better though. If Melanie had made up her mind to see Ross again, nothing Lil could do would prevent it. She could only postpone it, at best.

…

When Ross put the receiver down, he went into his bedroom, took a suitcase from the closet and threw in a change of clothes. Then he went into the bathroom and added some personals. He left the house and got into his car. Melanie waited in her parked car in front of his house. When she saw Ross get into his car, she pulled away. He started his vehicle and followed along behind her.

…

It was nearly six o'clock when they reached Regional Children's Hospital on the outskirts of Raleigh. They found parking places close together on the same level of the parking deck. A cold front had come through during the day, and it brought with it blustery winter winds that carried an Arctic chill. It blew

Melanie off balance, as it howled through the cement parking deck. Ross took her arm to steady her as they hurried to take the garage elevator to the hospital's main entrance.

When they reached the fifth floor, Ross followed Melanie to room 532. She walked into the room and over to the crib at the far side of the room. Ross watched from the doorway, as Melanie lowered the side rail and leaned over the child. Two chubby little arms reached up to embraced her.

"Mommy! You're back!"

"Just like I promised, Keri," Melanie said, kissing her cheek. "And, I've brought someone with me." Melanie stood up and looked behind her, then back at her child. "Keri, this is Ross. His name is Harrington, too. He wanted to meet you."

Ross moved to the side of the crib. He held his hand out to the golden haired, blue eyed toddler who looked to be between two and three. "Your mommy tells me you've been a pretty sick little girl," he said, smiling down at the child.

"Keri all better now," she told him. Her voice was a little raspy and her breathing still sounded wheezy from her illness. She looked at her mother for reassurance. "Mommy? You take me home with you, now?"

"Well sweetheart, you are much better," Melanie told her. "But, don't you remember what we talked about yesterday? You need to stay here, with Dr. Nick, for just a couple more days."

Keri stuck her lower lip out in a little pout. Melanie kissed her cheek, and the little girl smiled at her mother. Then, she reached for a stuffed teddy bear and hugged it to her. The child began to sing softly into the stuffed bear's ear.

Ross's heart went out to her. He looked at Melanie, "You're right, Mel. She is beautiful."

...

It was pushing eleven when Ross left Raleigh the following morning. He had intended to get an early start back to Serenity but had forgotten to leave a wake-up call. He'd been surprised when he opened his eyes to the bright ten o'clock morning sun. He'd been exhausted when he checked into the motel with a carryout chicken sandwich and chocolate malt for his evening meal. After eating, he had stretched across the bed to relax for a few minutes. The next thing he was aware of was the bright sunlight, as he opened his eyes the following morning.

He stopped for a ham-and-egg biscuit and coffee on the way out of town. He tried to call Lil, to let her know he expected to be there within the hour, but both lines were busy. "I need to hire another pharmacist," he thought aloud. It was ridiculous that he hadn't done so before. His life was becoming much too complicated, and the town's population was growing too. It was unfair to him, as well as his customers, for him not to do so.

As he drove, he pondered the last twenty-four hours. What a shock to hear from Melanie after all this time! He hadn't been sure what she was after when she said she had to see him. And, he had dreaded coming face to face with her. He had to admit she looked wonderful; time had improved her, and she was beautiful to begin with. And unexpectedly, she seemed to have changed. This woman who wanted to be footloose and fancy-free when she was married to him, who had said she never wanted children, that she wasn't cut out to be a mother, looked to be a very loving and devoted mother to Keri.

Ross had to admit his skepticism when she told him she had a child, but, upon seeing the little girl, there was no doubt left in his mind. She was a miniature version of Melanie.

What had really thrown him was what she said to him over lunch. "I was a fool to ever leave you, Ross. I didn't deserve you then. But, in the years we've been apart, I've found myself thinking of you more and more and what we could have had if I hadn't thrown it all away. I still love you, Ross. I'd like for us to try again." There had been tears in her eyes as she gently laid her hand over his. He'd been so overwhelmed that he couldn't find words immediately. He had sat there, in the sandwich shop, speechless, staring back at her.

When she told him about the child, she had been honest. She wasn't sure if it was his or Richard's. Richard had promised to marry her when she left Ross, but he was a married man. When he learned she was pregnant shortly after she left Ross, he told her he couldn't afford to leave his wife and didn't want any more children. He already had three, and the oldest was starting college at the time. At forty-two, he told her, he was too old to start over with a baby. They had gone their separate ways. She had taken a job in a medical laboratory to support herself and her baby. And, she had, as she put it, "done a great deal of growing up since becoming Keri's mother." She told Ross she wanted more children.

"Who in Serenity, of those who knew Melanie, would ever have guessed something like this?" he wondered aloud. It was a total about face.

Fifteen minutes later, Ross pulled in behind the drugstore, parked his car and went in through the rear door. He stepped into the pharmacy and donned his lab coat. Lil immediately came bustling from the front of the store to join him.

"Morning, Lil, would you please call Doc's office and get Maggie for me? I need to talk to her."

"She ain't there, Ross," Lil said curtly. "Maggie saw you and Melanie at the diner after you cancelled lunch with her. Doc had to send her home yesterday afternoon on account of her blood pressure went sky high, and he's worried about her and the baby. And by the way..."

"Oh my God," he cut her off. Ross turned and raced out of the drugstore without another word. He got into his car, and Lil heard the tires screech as he pulled away.

...

Ross turned into the Keller's driveway and parked behind Charlie's car. He got out quickly and climbed the steps to Maggie's apartment two at a time. He rang the bell and waited. "Maggie, are you in there? It's Ross. Let me in! I have to talk to you."

He waited a moment more then turned and raced back down the stairs. He went to the Keller's back door and rang the bell. When that got no results, he banged impatiently on the wooden frame. Ross could hear Charlie's voice inside as he heard the door lock release.

"Hold your horses. I'm coming." The door swung open. "Ross!"

"Lil told me Maggie was sent home yesterday. She doesn't answer her door. Is she here?"

"She is," Charlie said quietly. "But she's resting now. She's been pretty upset."

"I didn't want this to happen. I have to see her Charlie! I have to see her now!"

Charlie opened the door wide, and Ross pushed in past him. He went into their living room where Caroline had risen from the sofa and was starting toward the kitchen.

"Caroline, I have to talk to Maggie." Ross sounded breathless.

"Ross Harrington, you sit down and compose yourself a minute before I let you go in there. Maggie's sleepin', so a minute or two won't make any difference. You need to calm down before you talk to her. Maggie's had enough excitement in the last two days. She doesn't need you goin' in there all upset."

"You're right, Caroline," he said taking a deep breath. "It's just that Lil told me that Maggie was in the sandwich shop yesterday and saw me with Melanie. She said Maggie was pretty upset. I have to talk to her. His breathing had slowed, and he sounded more controlled.

"Caroline," Maggie called from the bedroom. "Do I hear Ross out there?"

Without hesitation, Ross hurried past Caroline and went into the bedroom. Maggie propped herself up on one elbow. Ross sat down on the side of her bed.

"Maggie, I'm so sorry. I didn't want to upset you. I've handled this all wrong." He embraced her and held her tightly to him. "I know you saw me with Melanie yesterday. Lil just told me. The last thing on earth I wanted to do was to hurt you. I should have told you when I cancelled with you that I was going to meet her. I was wrong not to. And now, by keeping it from you, I've only made matters worse."

Maggie looked into Ross's eyes waiting for him to continue. Her heart was beating rapidly. Did she want to hear what he had to say next? She wasn't sure.

Chapter Twenty-Two

"I love you, Maggie. I love you. I'm so sorry I've upset you." He pulled her to him. His lips brushed the tears rolling down her cheeks, the side of her neck and ended on her lips. "Can you forgive me for the way I've handled this?"

She pulled back from him until they were face to face. Her fingers traced his cheekbone. "I forgive you, Ross, but are you absolutely sure of this, of your feelings for Melanie?"

He kissed her again. "I'm absolutely sure, Maggie. You're the one I love, the one I want to spend the rest of my life with. It seemed strange to be with Melanie again after all this time and to look into her eyes and feel nothing but sympathy for the situation she's in. For a long time after she left, I couldn't imagine that I'd ever stop loving her and hurting because I'd lost her. But yesterday, being with her and feeling nothing, all I could think of was that I wanted to get back to Serenity and you, to tell you all that had happened."

Maggie leaned forward and kissed him.

"In the future, let's not hold anything back from one

another, no matter what it is. Deal?" He asked.

"Deal," she agreed. After all, she'd kept information from Ross too.

Maggie relayed the details of Michael's call. "Do you think he could get my child or even visitation rights?"

"Not after what I found out yesterday. But let me start with Melanie since I handled that so poorly. "Melanie called me at the pharmacy the night I returned from my meeting with Kevin. I've got to admit it was unnerving to hear her voice again. She said she had to talk to me. I told her to call me at the house later in the evening. She reached me about ten-thirty."

He went on to fill her in on everything that had transpired in the last twenty-four hours. Maggie listened without interruption.

"And you're absolutely certain of the way you feel about her proposal?"

"There's no way I'd even consider it, Maggie. I love you. I want to marry you just as soon as possible. Nothing has changed that. But, I do want to know if Keri's my daughter. And I've been giving it a good deal of thought since last night after I left them and driving back today. It doesn't really matter whether she's mine or not. I want to set up a fund for Keri, so that her education will be taken care of. I certainly have the means to do that. I inherited my home and some money from my grandparents, and I make good money at the pharmacy. Melanie doesn't have good insurance, and this hospital stay was expensive. I'd like to help her out with that, too."

"I understand, Ross. You do what you feel is right." She silently offered a prayer of thanks for the outcome of the last twenty-four hours.

There was a knock on the bedroom door. "You all right, Maggie?" Caroline called. "Doc's on the phone checkin' up on you."

"I didn't even hear the phone ring," Ross said on his

way to open the door. Caroline popped her head into the room smiling.

"Tell Doc I'm feeling much better now," Maggie told her grinning.

"I already did. He says he'll be by to check your blood pressure on his way home anyway." She stepped back into the living room closing their door as she did.

Ross sat back down on the side of Maggie's bed. "And now for Mr. Kevin Williams and the good doctor. You'll like this, Maggie." He began to chuckle. "When I showed up, Kevin told his secretary to tell me he was tied up for the entire day, that he didn't have time to see me. I let myself into his office against the secretary's protests, and there sits Mr. Williams, feet propped on his desk, reading John Grisham's latest paperback."

Maggie couldn't suppress her laughter. "Oh, Ross, you're joking!"

He held up his right hand. "Scouts honor," he said, feigning a sober expression. "Anyway, the woman was about to call security on me when I mentioned to Kevin that I'd recently met with Calvin Whitton. He immediately became considerably more cooperative."

"I'll bet he did."

Ross continued, "To begin with, he was very cautious about the way he worded everything. But when I pulled out the letter and told him that it was a copy of the original that was in a safe-deposit box and that Mr. Whitton was willing to testify that he represented himself as your attorney, he broke down and told me how he became involved.

"Lee General is a client of the law firm Kevin works for. It seems one of the senior partners is the brother-in-law of the chairman of the board of directors at the hospital. Shortly after Kevin joined the firm, he was assigned as a member of the legal team that handled that account. He traveled to Alexandria several times and met Michael on one of his first trips. He says this all began before you were in the picture. Anyway, they hit it off and used to go up to Atlantic City for weekends to gamble and meet women. To hear Kevin tell it, Michael was a real womanizer."

"And obviously hasn't changed," Maggie said, rolling her eyes.

"Well, Michael had a turn of bad luck at the tables and lost upwards of two hundred thousand dollars to the casino. He second mortgaged his house and borrowed money to pay the casino off, then started day trading over the Internet to try to recoup his losses. He was losing more than winning and had to borrow more money to keep trading. Because he was so desperate, he made some pretty risky investments and ended up compounding his losses. Because he became desperate, he began filing fraudulent tax returns. He borrowed money from several private sources. Kevin says he loaned him money up to a point, but Michael was draining him, too. So, he agreed to take Michael on as a client and try to work out some repayment terms with the government in order to keep him out of prison."

"Oh, my gosh. That's incredible! Michael seems to have a whole side to him that I hadn't a clue about. They must be some kind of friends for Kevin to loan him that kind of money."

"What Kevin said, was that during the time they were going to Atlantic City frequently, Michael did Kevin a tremendous favor. He wouldn't elaborate, but, because of it, Kevin felt obligated to loan him the money. As the situation progressed, I suppose Kevin felt the only hope he would have of ever recouping any of his own losses was to agree to help Michael in his negotiations with the IRS.

"He also agreed to do what he could to help Michael try to get you back. I suppose Michael promised him some cash if it worked out. Michael was following the airline's lawsuit in the papers up there, and he figured, if you and he were married, it would go a long way toward solving his financial problems."

Maggie listened, spellbound.

"Now, Kevin's terrified that if we make an issue of his involvement, he'll be severely reprimanded by the state law board. He would, in all probability, lose his job. He'd probably be disbarred."

"It would certainly be interesting to know just what that favor was. It had to have been immense for Kevin to risk his law career," Maggie said.

"Several possibilities come to mind," Ross replied.

"Hmm, you think you know someone," Maggie mused.

"By the time I left, Kevin was on his second helping of humble pie. Says he deeply regrets getting involved in the whole thing. He, of course, hopes we'll let his part in this drop, and he promised he'd try to talk some sense into Michael."

"I wonder if he can, if anyone can at this point. You know, as I think of it, Robyn's great uncle died last year. She always said he was quite a wealthy man. She was one of the beneficiaries of his will. For a while, she talked about it at great length. She used to take her afternoon break with Michael and me. I suppose that's when it all started between them. It must not have been as much as he needed, because they didn't stay together long. That must have been what she meant when she said she didn't have enough."

"I don't know, Maggie. I don't know what to make of a man like that. Michael sounds to me like he needs some psychiatric care. He also needs a financial counselor as well as a good tax attorney."

Maggie shook her head. "What a mess! How desperate Michael must feel. A gambling addiction is a terrible thing. I wonder what other surprises he has for us before this all ends. I'll have to say, I think he'd have a hard time convincing any court that he'd be more fit to raise my child than I would."

"I agree. I'm sorry for the way he's hurt you. I hate that you had to go through it. But how lucky for you to be out of that whole situation. And I'll be eternally grateful for your feeling the need to stretch your legs that morning at the Serenity exit." He leaned forward and took her in his arms.

"Me, too, Ross. Me, too."

...

Doc and Kathryn came by at five-thirty. Kathryn visited with Caroline and Charlie, while Doc went into the bedroom to check on Maggie.

Doc took her pressure twice, while Ross sat on the side of the bed. "Steady as can be at 116 over 74 now. Ross, son, don't do anything like this again. For heaven's sake, call Maggie, and talk to her first."

"You're absolutely right. I stand duly chastised. Believe me, I've already told Maggie that's how it'll be in the future."

"I told her there was a logical explanation for you not telling her, and obviously you've cleared it up for her because she looks fit as a fiddle now. And, Maggie, your urinalysis results came out fine."

"That's wonderful," she said softly as she leaned against Ross.

"I'll have to admit you caused me a lot of concern young lady, but all's well that ends well. Now, I want you to get some good sleep tonight, and it might not be a bad idea to have someone with you for the night. If I were you, I'd stay right here with Caroline and Charlie."

"Thanks, Doc. I'll probably do just that."

After the Millers left, Maggie and Ross went into the living room and visited with Caroline and Charlie. Caroline fixed dinner for them, but after dinner Maggie and Ross left and went up to Maggie's apartment.

...

The aroma of fresh coffee greeted Maggie's nostrils as she awakened the following morning. She heard the refrigerator door open and, a few seconds later, the sizzle of bacon frying in a skillet. The hickory smoked smell made her mouth water as it drifted into the bedroom.

By the time she got up and reached the kitchen, Ross had their breakfast nearly ready. "You're just the kind of husband material I've been looking for all my life. Will you marry me, Ross Harrington?" She kissed him before going to her seat at the table.

"I thought you'd never ask, Maggie Thornton. Just set the date." He placed a plate of bacon, scrambled eggs and toast in front of her, leaned down and kissed her. "And make it soon," he added.

"This looks wonderful. I'm starving!" She took a sip of decaf.

Ross carried his plate to the table and sat down across from her. "I'm serious, Maggie. I want you to talk to Reverend Townlee today."

"I will, Ross. And we have a lot of decisions to make in a short time. I know we want to keep it small and simple, but we do need to decide on who we want to stand up with us. Have you given that any thought?"

"I have. I'm going to ask Doc to be my best man—for lots of reasons," he added seriously.

Maggie nodded. "I can't leave Caroline or Lil out, and I have to find a position of equal importance for both. Of course, I want my aunts to attend. And Ross, what do you think of asking Bobby Hensley to be our ring bearer?"

"Perfect. I think Bobby would absolutely love it. But we'll have to insist on no spiders in the church."

Maggie laughed. "I'll leave that up to you."

"And, of course, I'll remind him that when Reverend Townlee says 'you may kiss the bride', that he's referring to me."

"Why, Ross, I think you're jealous." She winked at him. "But, you're right. The first thing we need to do is talk to Reverend Townlee and see when he's available, and when we can have the church."

At noon, Maggie called the rectory. Marion Townlee answered the phone. "Just a minute, Maggie. I'll get him for you. I was about to call him for lunch anyway."

Maggie could hear her in the distance as she summoned her husband. Reverend Townlee seemed delighted when Maggie told him what she wanted.

"Can you hold a minute, Maggie Thornton? I'll take a look at the church calendar?" It took him only a moment. "How does three weeks from next Saturday sound to you?"

"Fantastic. I'm sure that will suit Ross. I just hope I can be ready by then. There's so much to do."

"Then I'm going to schedule you in. It's about time, young lady."

After Maggie hung up she wondered what he meant by that. Was he referring to the baby? She lifted the receiver again and dialed the pharmacy. Ross picked up, and she relayed the date to him.

"That's terrific, Maggie-almost-Harrington."

Maggie could hear Lil in the background. Then she got on the phone with Maggie.

"Good for you two! Congratulations, and I'll help you anyway I can, Maggie."

"I know you will, Lil. We'll get together and start planning soon."

"I'm gonna put Ross back on now. Bye."

Maggie and Ross talked for a few more minutes. When they hung up, Maggie called Caroline and Charlie. They were thrilled at the news and excited at the special part they'd have in this ceremony. Maggie asked Charlie to stand in for her father and give her away. Caroline and Lil would be the directors. Caroline also wanted to help with some of the food preparation.

As the week progressed, there were no surprises for Maggie or Ross. They were both grateful, because recently, as Maggie said, "We've had enough surprises to hold us clear through our golden anniversary."

Everything continued smoothly through the weekend. On Monday, Ross and Maggie had lunch together. "I'm going to call Melanie and see if she'll agree to a paternity test. It nags at me, and I want to know. How do you feel about that, Maggie?"

"I think you should do what you feel you have to, Ross. I can certainly understand your feelings."

"I think I'll call Melanie tonight. She gave me her number. Do you want to be there when I talk to her?"

"No. I think that's between the two of you."

...

Ross and Melanie spoke several times over the next couple days. Keri was at home again and seemed to have fully recovered from her bout with double pneumonia.

Melanie agreed to the testing, and the appointment was scheduled. Ross and Melanie made arrangements to meet at the end of the week at Duke. Blood would be drawn from both Ross and Keri for an HLA test that would determine the genetic make-up of both; thus giving Ross, as positively as could be determined, the answer to his question. When everything had been finalized on Wednesday, Ross phoned Maggie. She picked up on the third ring.

"Hello."

"Darling, I've just hung up with Melanie. We're set for Friday at Duke. Eleven in the morning. Will you go with me?"

Though she felt a little pang inside, Maggie hesitated only a moment as one of her mother's favorite adages came to mind. *Hold fast with open arms.* "No. I think this is something between you and Melanie. I'll stay here. Plan to have dinner with me if you're back in time."

"Are you sure, honey?"

"I'm sure. I love you. I hope you understand why I'm not going with you."

"I do. I love you, too. I'll see you as soon as I get back."

...

Friday morning Ross was up before the sun rose. He hadn't slept well the night before. In fact, he had tossed and turned most of the night, as his mind kept replaying all that had happened recently.

He had mixed emotions as to how he wanted the test results to turn out. On one hand he found himself hoping to learn that he had a daughter. On the other, perhaps it would be better were she not his child. He had missed so much of her short life. He hated to think that he had a child who's birth he had missed, and all the special achievements in her life; her first smile, her first little sounds, her first laugh out loud, her first steps. He closed his eyes for a moment then redirected his thoughts.

He wondered if today would be busy at the pharmacy. He was relieved that Ryan Johnson had agreed to come on board at the drugstore. The customers had all liked him when he had filled in both in the past and again last week. For some time, Ryan had wanted to move back to Serenity. He had relatives in town, and he was dating Diane Summers, the librarian in Serenity. So, he had been quick to accept Ross's offer.

...

Friday at 9:15 A.M., Ross set off for Durham. He made good time and arrived with thirty minutes to spare. He stopped at the information desk and got directions to the lab. To his surprise, he found that Melanie and Keri were already there when he checked in.

Melanie looked very patriotic in royal blue slacks, white turtleneck and a red fleece jacket. Ross thought her quite stunning. Melanie had always worn clothes well. In the past, he'd often thought that she could make even a pair of faded blue jeans look elegant.

As soon as Keri saw Ross, she ran to him. "Hi, Ross," she said loudly. Her voice was clear today, and her eyes shone a very bright blue. As she reached him, she wrapped her arms about his legs.

He felt his heart melt. "Hi, Keri. How's my girl? " he heard himself ask.

"All well. Keri home now." she grinned so broadly her little eyes crinkled shut.

"Good for you, Keri. I'm glad you're all better."

Melanie smiled, stepped up to Ross and gave him a little hug.

...

When the tests were completed Melanie asked Ross to have lunch with her and Keri.

They went to TGI Friday's. Melanie told him it was one of Keri's favorites. She loved their chicken fingers. Keri chattered almost incessantly during lunch, and Ross only understood about half of what she said. But he found himself becoming enchanted with the little girl. By the end of lunch, Keri was getting tired. She ended up on her mother's lap. Within moments, she fell asleep. Ross walked with Melanie to her car and waited while she strapped the sleeping child into her car seat.

"I guess we'll know something in a week or so, Mel," he said softly.

"Uh-huh. I guess we will."

"Well, I'll say good-bye now, Melanie. You're doing a super job at this mom business. I'm really proud of you." He turned and started over to his car.

"Ross," she called softly.

He stopped and turned back toward her.

She ran to him and wrapped her arms about his neck. "I don't want you to leave us. Have you thought any more about what I said to you at the hospital last week?"

"Melanie," he said softly.

She pressed her lips against his and held him tightly.

Chapter Twenty-Three

"Melanie," Ross repeated her name more firmly. He took a step back and held her at arm's length. "There's someone else. I'm very much in love with her. We're going to be married soon."

"Then, it's really true," she stammered.

"What? What's true?"

"Oh...oh nothing." She spoke haltingly. "That... that you can't recapture the past. That you can't go back, Ross."

"I guess that's right. We just have to keep pushing forward. You certainly have, Mel. You've come such a long way. You've grown, and I'm proud of you. I'll always be here for you if you need any help with Keri, regardless of how the test comes out. I hope we can be friends."

"Well, we'll see. How do you think Maggie would feel about that?"

"She's a wonderful girl, Mel. She loves kids and feels the same as I do about this."

They had parted with those words. Melanie walked to

her car without looking back, and Ross left Durham and headed to Serenity.

He seemed to have been on the road more lately than he'd been home. He hoped this trip was the end of it until he and Maggie left on their honeymoon. With that thought, he was reminded that they hadn't even discussed a trip. Nor had they shopped for rings! He needed to get back to Maggie and get on with their arrangements. It was sure great to know that Ryan was in the pharmacy taking care of business for him.

As he drove along, his mind replayed his and Melanie's parting. What a relief these last months not to feel a longing to see her face or feel her touch. Then to see her again and feel nothing when she embraced him and kissed him. And to wake each morning and go to sleep each night with thoughts of only Maggie.

"Maggie!" He said aloud as it struck him. Melanie had asked what *Maggie* would think of it. He hadn't mentioned her by name, but Melanie had known. She had called her Maggie!

Chapter Twenty-Four

The following days were filled with working and planning. On Friday, Ross and Maggie drove to Fayetteville to choose their wedding rings. They went to several jewelry stores before making a decision. Ross wanted to buy Maggie a diamond engagement and wedding set, but she preferred a simple gold band.

"Maybe for a twenty-fifth anniversary, or I may even want to wait for fifty. I expect to be in your life for a very long time," she said teasingly. "But, in all honestly, Ross, I wouldn't be able to wear it at the clinic. I'm always pulling rubber gloves on and off. And, that's most of the time, so let's wait on the diamonds."

"That makes pretty good sense." They agreed upon his and hers gold bands with a platinum diamond cut pattern etched through the center. Under the jeweler's lights, it glittered brilliantly giving the illusion of little diamond sets. Before they left, Ross asked the jeweler to engrave Maggie's.

"While we're here would you like to shop for a wedding dress, Maggie?"

"Might as well. I can't put it off much longer, or I'll be wearing my uniform," she said with a laugh. "How about you? Do you need to look for anything?"

"I have an old tux. Believe it or not, it's ten years old but still fits. I can wear that or a suit, whichever you prefer."

"Let's see what I find, then you can decide which you prefer. You're not afraid this will jinx us are you? Picking it out together, I mean?"

"I'm not superstitious, are you?"

She reached up and kissed him. "Not in the least."

...

He sat in one of the several chairs in the formal wear department of Dillard's in the mall. He thought back to her remark about being jinxed. With all that had been going on in their lives the last couple of months, did he even dare to expect that the wedding would go smoothly? That all the surprises were behind them?

...

With only a few days left before their wedding, everything was falling into place nicely except for one thing. Ross hadn't received the results of the paternity test yet, but he expected to hear any day.

When Maggie arrived home Monday evening, she reached into the mailbox and removed several envelopes. She glanced through them quickly. "Looks like mostly junk mail," she commented absent-mindedly. "How do these folks always manage to find me no matter where I go?" As she tucked the mail against her chest, a yellow slip of paper dropped to the ground. She glanced at it. It was an attempt to deliver a piece of registered mail. Her stomach did a little flip.

Oh, dear Lord, now what? she wondered. She glanced at her watch. It was too late to pick it up today; the post office closed fifteen minutes ago.

Chapter Twenty-Five

Maggie phoned the post office as soon as it opened the next morning. She recognized the voice of the man who answered the call. "Clarence, this is Maggie Thornton," she said.

"I know. Mornin'. What can I do for you today?"

"I had a notice in my mailbox yesterday that you have a registered letter for me. Would you please hold it there at the post office, and I'll pick it up a little later this morning? Oh, and Clarence," she added as an after thought, "would you mind checking and telling me who it's from?"

"I will if you can hold a minute," he said. He returned to the phone within minutes. "Maggie, I don't see it here just now. I'm gonna have to track down the carrier. I wonder if Bud's already packed it up with his regular deliveries. But it seems to me that yesterday, he said it was from some law firm in Virginia, if I'm rememberin' right."

Good old small town, everybody knows your business, she thought. "Thanks. On second thought, if you can catch Bud before he leaves the post office, would you please ask him to drop it by the clinic instead of the house?"

...

At ten-thirty, Maggie's registered letter was delivered to her at work. She breathed a sigh of relief as soon as she saw the return address. She had felt it was nothing to worry about when the postmaster told her it was from a Virginia law firm. Still, she was relieved to see that the return address was Whitton, White and Weston and not connected to Michael in any way.

She went back to the break room and opened the envelope. Mr. Whitton had written her a letter and enclosed was a check for two-million-one-hundred-thousand dollars, written on the firm's escrow account. It was even more than she had expected. Maggie's hand trembled as she clutched the slip of gray paper. *I must get this deposited in a safe place and soon*, she thought. She reached for the phone on the desk and dialed the pharmacy.

"R.H. Pharmacy. How can I help you?"

"Hi, Lil. Is Ross in?"

"He is, honey. You all right today?" she asked. "You sound a little excited."

"I'm fine, Lil. I just need to talk to Ross."

"He'll be with you in a minute."

Very shortly, Maggie heard Ross's voice. "Hi, Honey."

"Hi! I just received the mail I've been expecting from Calvin Whitton. It was delivered to me here at the office by registered mail. Now I need to decide where to put it. Let's go to lunch. My treat. You can order anything or everything on the menu." She laughed, then added, "The sky's the limit."

...

At twelve-thirty, Maggie removed her purse from her locker and started to leave the clinic. She got as far the front desk when Sarah Hensley burst through the front door. She was hysterical, her face was scarlet. "Matt's having chest… he's got pain! And his arm…" she sobbed. "I'm afraid it's his heart!"

Maggie dropped her bag on the reception desk. "Mildred, please lock this in your file cabinet for me," she said as she went to Sarah. "Where is Matt?" she asked calmly.

"He's in the car, he couldn't…please help him, Maggie."

"Mildred," Maggie's voice was controlled. "Please get Doc. Tell him what Sarah said, and ask him to come out to the car and help me with Matt. Then take Sarah into one of the empty rooms and stay with her, please."

Mildred disappeared into the back, and Maggie went outside. She opened the door on the passenger side of the Hensley's car. Matt was in a semi-prone position with his eyes closed. Maggie loosened the tightly buttoned collar of his shirt. Doc was at Maggie's side within seconds. Matt was conscious, but he was perspiring profusely, and his face was ashen. One had only to glance at him to recognize that he was in severe pain. He struggled for each breath.

"Matt. Can you hear me?" Doc asked calmly.

"Yes," he whispered. "It's bad, Doc, real bad." He winced between gasps.

"I'm going to give you an injection, Matt. But first, I want you to chew these baby aspirins for me. Can you do that?"

He struggled to answer. "Uh huh."

Doc removed the lid from the bottle he held and slid two little tablets into Matt's mouth then recapped the bottle and dropped it back into his pocket.

Matt dutifully chewed the aspirin.

Kathryn arrived at the car with a Gurney.

A few moments later, Matt had been wheeled into one of the examining rooms, the injection was beginning to take effect, and he was resting a bit more comfortably. Minutes later, an ambulance arrived to transport him to Cape Fear Hospital in Fayetteville. Doc asked Kathryn to drive Sarah home with orders to rest and take one of the sedatives he sent home with her.

When the excitement was over, Maggie went back to Mildred's desk to pick up her purse and leave to meet Ross for lunch.

"Oh yes," Mildred said. "I was supposed to tell you. Ross called from the sandwich shop to see where you were. I filled him in on our emergency but said it shouldn't be much longer. He said he'd wait there for you."

"Thanks, Mildred. Now, if you'll get me my purse, I'll be on my way. I'll try to be back within thirty minutes."

Mildred looked around her. "I don't have your purse, Maggie."

"But I asked you to put it in your file cabinet for me. I left it on your desk when I went out to Matt." She could feel her blood pressure rising. She forced herself to take a deep breath.

"I'm sorry, Maggie, I didn't hear you. I was so intent on Sarah." Mildred looked around her desk area then checked her file drawer. "Nothing here. Oh Maggie, I'm so sorry," she repeated. They both looked about Mildred's office and the waiting room. The purse was nowhere to be found!

Maggie felt faint. She sank into Mildred's desk chair. "I can't believe this," she murmured. "Who was in the waiting room?"

The picture of the stranger from the church flashed into Maggie's mind, and her heart sank even lower. Had there been a stranger in the office today? She couldn't even recall who was there when she went with Sarah. She had been so concerned for Matt. Was she being paranoid now? She hoped so. But so much had happened lately. No, she couldn't give in to this suspicion. Surely the purse would turn up. She couldn't believe that any of their patients would stoop so low, as to knowingly take it. Ross, she had to see Ross. He'd help her sort this out.

Mildred looked alarmed. "Maggie," she said, shaking her shoulder gently. "Maggie, you're as white as fresh snow. Do I need to call Doc for you?"

"No, Mildred. I'll be all right. I need to see Ross." She rose and walked to the clinic door before stopping. "I don't have keys for my car."

"I'll call down to the sandwich shop and ask Ross to pick you up, honey," Mildred offered, lifting the receiver.

"He's going to think I'm a fool," her whisper audible only to herself. To Mildred, she managed a faint, "Thanks."

A few minutes later, Ross pulled up in front of the clinic. Maggie ran out and got into his car. "Oh, Ross, you aren't going to believe what I've done."

"What *have* you done, Maggie?" he asked with exaggerated drama.

"I've lost my purse! And, with it, the check, my keys, everything!"

"That's not a funny joke, Maggie." One look at her, and his expression became as grave as hers. "You aren't kidding, are you?"

"I wish I were."

How?"

Maggie quickly relayed the details of the last thirty-five minutes. "Mildred's calling the few people who were still in the waiting room when Sarah came in to see if they can shed any light on what happened."

"Well, in the meantime, I think it might be wise to notify Calvin Whitton. The best course of action would probably be to ask him to stop payment on that check immediately and issue you another."

"You're right, of course. But I feel so totally stupid having to call and tell him that I barely kept track of it for an hour."

"Do you want me to call for you?" he offered.

"No. I'm the one who lost it. I'll do it myself. And, I need to do it now. Let's go back to my apartment, and I'll get my other set of car keys. Uh-oh. If Charlie or Caroline aren't home I can't even get into my apartment."

"Let's go by and see, Maggie."

Maggie hadn't noticed that Ross had pulled away from the curb and was already halfway there. When he reached the Kellers' house, he pulled into the driveway. Charlie's car was gone.

"I'll ring the bell. Caroline may be at home," Maggie said, opening her car door. She stepped to the door and rang several times. No one answered. Maggie got back into the car looking dejected.

Ross said, "Let's go to the drugstore and get the number from information. You can talk to Mr. Whitton from there. I'll keep Lil occupied, so you have privacy."

"Okay," she said, glancing at her watch. "I hope he's in the office today and not at lunch or tied up in court. That would be just my luck, the way this day is going."

When they reached the drugstore, Ross asked Lil to help him in the stock room and closed Maggie in the pharmacy. She got the number from information but decided to check with Mildred before dialing Mr. Whitton.

"I wish I had some good news for you, Maggie, but I don't," Mildred told her as soon as she heard Maggie's voice. "The only folks who were still here were Bea Anderson and Cletus Baker, and neither of them saw anything. Bea said she was so busy watching the goings on and the paramedics carting Matt out of here that she didn't pay any attention to anything else. And then Cletus, being a man and all, just said, 'Nope, didn't see nothin'."

It was a relief to know that those two were the only ones in the office at the time, at least as far as Mildred knew. "Thanks. I'll be back as soon as I make one more call,

Mildred. Bye."

She broke the connection then dialed Calvin Whitton's number. Her heart raced as she waited. When the receptionist answered, she told Maggie that Calvin Whitton wasn't in but was expected to be back by mid-afternoon.

Maggie's spirits took another nose-dive. "It's crucial that I speak with him. Would you please ask him to contact me as soon as he comes in?"

"I will. Please give me a number where you can be reached."

Maggie gave her the number for the clinic, as well as the number at her apartment, should it be late when he returned the call.

...

When Maggie entered the clinic, Mildred was all smiles. "I tried to reach you at the sandwich shop and the pharmacy. Lil said you were on your way back here. Good news! I've had a call from the paramedic services, and they have your purse. They picked it up with some of their stuff, it bein' black and all."

"Hallelujah!" Maggie sank down into a waiting room chair.

"They're gonna drop it by on their way back through town. They said they thought it would be sometime before five," she said glancing at her watch.

...

By 4:45 P.M. Maggie had her purse back, and, other than her billfold being unsnapped, nothing else seemed to have been disturbed. The check was still in the envelope it had been mailed in. She breathed a deep sigh of relief.

She called Ross to let him know that another disaster

had been averted. Then, since she hadn't heard from Mr. Whitton, she called his office and told his secretary she no longer needed to speak with him.

...

Their evening was devoted to wedding plans. Even a small, simple event often turns out to be more complicated as one actually gets into making the arrangements. Theirs was no exception. Caroline would hear of no one other than herself baking the wedding cake. Carl and his wife had offered to cater the small reception that was growing by the day as the word spread of the pending marriage. As patients were seen and conversation turned to the marriage, Maggie found herself inviting one after another.

Ross and Maggie stayed after the church service the previous Sunday to go over the chapel arrangements with Reverend Townlee. At that time, Maggie asked Marion Townlee to play the organ.

"That sounds lovely," Marion had said, when they gave her their selections. "I've always thought 'The Gift of Love' one of the most appropriate, and you could never make a better choice than 'The Lord's Prayer'."

They stopped by Reverend Townlee's home briefly this Sunday evening. As they rose to leave, he said, "So you think there'll be about forty guests, give or take a few, is that right?"

"Oh, no. I don't think that *is* right," Maggie said. Let's see; there are my two aunts, of course, and Charlie, Caroline and Lil. Then, there's Bobby Hensley, our ring bearer and his parents. Matt wants to come if he's up to it, but Sarah says she'll be there either way. Add Doc, Kathryn and Mildred, plus the patients. I've invited at least thirty, so far, along with their families."

Ross interrupted, "You've been inviting patients? I've invited a few folks when they came in down at the drugstore, too."

By the time they had finished the tally, to date there were over one hundred and twenty guests. "And that's with almost a week to go." Ross couldn't suppress a grin.

"I guess there's no such thing as a small, intimate wedding in a small, intimate community like Serenity," Maggie chimed in.

"It looks that way," Ross said. "We're all something of a family, so it's hard to leave anyone out when you start making guest lists, isn't it?"

"You're right about that. And from the way things are going, I think this affair is going to keep growing," Reverend Townlee added. "But, where are we going to put everyone for the reception? This isn't summer weather where we can spill over into the churchyard."

"Now don't you bother yourself about that," Marion chided. "You just leave that part to the women. We'll manage. There's always room for one more when there's a happy occasion bein' blessed by the Lord."

"You're right as usual, my dear," her husband said, winking at Ross. Then to Ross he added, "You'd better memorize that line, son. And do it soon, because it will serve you well and often in the years to come."

When Ross and Maggie left the Townlee's, they drove to Maggie's. "Before we go upstairs, I think I should stop in and let Caroline know how this event is growing."

Charlie let them in. They sat around the kitchen table as they chatted.

"My idea is to bake a four-tier wedding cake and a couple of large pan cakes, too. I'll decorate them all the same, and that should be plenty," Caroline said as if she were thinking out loud. "I already have the tiers in the freezer, but I still have the flat cakes to bake. I'll do all the decorating early Friday."

"That sounds wonderful. What would I do without you two and Lil?" Maggie asked.

"It's our pleasure, Maggie. Lil and I have been talking

every day at least twice. You don't need to worry. Everything's under control."

"I know, Caroline. But we do need to give Carl and Irene an accurate count."

"I'll take care of that too, honey. You don't need to worry yourself about it."

...

Ross and Maggie left and started across the lawn to Maggie's apartment. "Oh, I almost forgot to tell you. My aunts are planning to fly now instead of drive, and I'm relieved. Aunt Clara says she can't do all the driving on such a long trip. And, Aunt Em is getting cataracts, so she doesn't trust her behind the wheel. They'll fly into the Raleigh-Durham airport on Friday, around noon. That means we have to find someone to pick them up."

"Why don't I go up? It would be a good chance to try to convince them that a pharmacist is every bit as honorable as that doctor they were so enamoured with."

Maggie burst out laughing. "You just landed yourself the job as chauffeur."

...

On Tuesday evening as Ross started out his front door to spend the evening with Maggie, his phone rang. He was tempted not to answer then thought better of it. When he heard the voice on the other end of the line, he wished he'd followed his first instinct.

Chapter Twenty-Six

"This is a warning. Don't try to go through with your wedding plans. It will never take place. Never!" The caller hung up.

The male voice had been very muffled as if the speaker portion of the phone was covered with something thick. It made identifying the caller's voice impossible. Ross lifted the receiver again and pressed *69 to see where the call had originated even though he expected it would be an exercise in futility. It was!

Ross took his wallet out of his pocket. He removed Kevin Williams' business card, picked up the phone and dialed his home number. The phone rang several times. Just as he was about to give up on Kevin, he heard his voice.

"Kevin. This is Ross Harrington."

"Yes, Ross. What can I do for you?" Kevin's tone was pleasant.

"I don't suppose you me called just a few minutes ago,"

"No, Ross. I didn't, but I had planned to call this evening. I just walked in the door as the phone was ringing.

What can I do for you?"

"Oh? Why were you going to call me?" Ross was curious, and what a change in Kevin's attitude since their meeting in Raleigh.

"I talked with Michael, as I promised. I think I got through to him that he needs to forget about Maggie and get on with his life, that she isn't the answer to his problems. I'm still working with him and the IRS. I've told him he has to stay on the straight and narrow if he wants me to continue representing him. I don't think you'll hear anything more out of him. Would you pass that on to Maggie for me, please?"

"Thanks, Kevin. I will." They hung up.

Ross lifted the receiver for the third time and dialed information in Alexandria, Virginia. He asked for Michael Kerns's number. He waited. Perhaps when Michael answered the phone there would be something in his voice that Ross might recognize from the call he'd had minutes before. He knew the chance was slim. Still, it was worth the try.

The operator came on the line. "I'm sorry, sir. That is an unpublished number."

Dead-end! Ross hung the receiver up, picked up his car keys and left his house. Though he'd promised no more secrets, he decided not to worry Maggie with the threatening call. She'd had enough concerns lately without adding this one. He couldn't help but wish he had the call on tape. Ah well, what he must do now is be very alert and watchful of any strangers who arrive on the scene, and he'd definitely stay close to Maggie. Perhaps he should talk to Charlie so he could keep his eyes open too. And, he'd take no chances. He was going to bring Sheriff Barton in on this.

...

By Wednesday, when Ross still had no word from Duke, he toyed with the idea of calling the lab directly. By noon, he still hadn't made the call. He planned to have lunch with Maggie at her apartment. She had taken two weeks vacation starting today. Ryan Johnson had moved to Serenity and started full time with him this past Monday freeing Ross up to be out of the pharmacy as much as needed.

"I won't be back unless you call me," Ross told Ryan as he took his lab jacket off. "You can reach me at Maggie's. Her number's on my Rolodex."

Ryan looked up from his work. "Enjoy yourself. We'll be just fine here. Hey, isn't that why you hired me?"

Ross had his hand on the doorknob when the phone rang. Ross hesitated for a moment until Ryan picked up. As Ross opened the door to leave, Ryan held up his index finger and motioned Ross to wait.

"Ross, can you take this call before you leave?" He asked, holding the receiver against his chest. "It's a woman. She says her name is Melanie, and that it's important."

Ross stepped back through the door and reached for the receiver. "Hello, Mel. What's up? Have you heard anything, yet?"

"As a matter of fact, that's what I was calling about. I just heard from Duke in my morning mail. Do you have yours yet?"

"I don't know. I haven't had a chance to check the mail at the house today. What does it show?"

"Can you meet me?"

Ross was silent

"Even half-way? I'll come halfway, Ross. We could meet in Pittsboro."

"Why, Mel? Why can't we talk about it on the phone?"

"Because, there's something I have to explain, Ross. And, something I have to warn you about."

Chapter Twenty-Seven

Ross and Maggie ate a quick lunch together before Ross headed to Pittsboro to meet Melanie. He had allowed himself an hour and ten minutes for the fifty-minute drive. Before leaving town, he wanted to stop by his place to check his mail. He preferred not to have any surprises when he met Melanie, however he wasn't sure what to expect in the form of the warning she spoke of on the phone.

There was no letter from Duke. Disappointed, he got back into the car and headed out toward Pittsboro. He couldn't help but wonder why he hadn't received word when Melanie had. Lately, it seemed the only mail he ever received was junk mail.

Fifteen minutes into the trip, traffic stopped. He sat patiently for a few moments, but, when traffic made no forward progress, several drivers in the cars ahead of him got out of their vehicles. After a short wait, Ross followed suit.

At first he saw nothing; there was no traffic coming from the opposite direction either. Then suddenly a horrific boom shook the ground beneath him and black smoke and flames billowed into the air. Within seconds, Ross heard sirens. A fire truck and ambulance made their way from behind him though traffic and toward the site of the accident. Ross could hear sirens coming from the opposite direction, too. He went back to his car and got in, his mind's eye forming images of what might lie ahead. The thought crossed his mind that someone who had kissed their loved one, or ones, good-bye this morning was probably going to have their life turned upside down this evening. He suddenly felt an overwhelming desire to hear Maggie's voice. He flipped open his cell phone and dialed her number, but the line was busy.

He sat for what seemed an interminable amount of time, glancing frequently between his watch and the clock on the dash. Thirty minutes passed, then Ross saw two wreckers weaving their way to the accident scene. That took another twenty minutes. Ross flipped his cell phone open and tried Maggie again. The line was still busy.

He decided he should try Melanie's home number. He didn't expect her to answer; she didn't. He left her a message in case he missed her this afternoon. At least she'd know what held him up. She didn't have a cell phone, so there was nothing more to do but wait until traffic began to move again and drive on to Pittsboro. For a fleeting instant, he wondered if Melanie could possibly have been involved in the collision.

Finally, cars ahead of Ross's began to creep forward. He started his engine and drove forward slowly. As he reached the site of the accident, the roadside grass looked blackened and barren; the guardrail was a twisted mass of metal, and there was shattered glass all along the roadside. He saw the crumpled mass of what had once been a red sports car still on the shoulder of the road, and the burned out cab of an overturned Semi still smoldered just beyond it. The wreckers were hard at work. Thank God, it wasn't a white car like Melanie drove. Ross shook his head and wondered if anyone had been fortunate enough to survive, and, as an after-thought, he wondered if survival really would be fortunate, considering the apparent destruction to the vehicles.

By the time he pulled into Pittsboro, he was more than an hour late. He drove down the main street and pulled into the shopping center wondering if Melanie would still be there. He spotted the drugstore where they had agreed to meet and slowly made his way to it. He looked for Melanie's car but didn't see it. He started to pull into a parking place when he thought he spied a car that looked like hers pulling out of the shopping area. He quickly turned his steering wheel and drove in her direction. She turned onto the main thoroughfare and drove on through the intersection. By the time Ross got onto the road the green light had turned yellow. He drove hurriedly through it then chided himself for his recklessness after what he had just witnessed.

He sped up until he was close enough to the car to see that it was Melanie. He began to blow his horn. He certainly wanted to catch her and find out what was so important that she had to tell him in person. The last thing he needed, or wanted, was to have to make another trip to learn whatever it was she had to say.

She seemed oblivious to his horn. Finally, he managed to pull into the lane beside her and get her attention. Both vehicles slowed, and he rolled the passenger window down and called to her.

"Sorry I'm late, Mel. Traffic was held up for an accident. It was a hell of a wreck."

"I was wondering what happened. There's a quiet little commons up a short way on the right. Let's talk there, Ross. Follow me."

He maneuvered back into traffic behind her. When they reached the park, they found a secluded stone bench under a shade tree not far from the parking area.

"Now. Tell me—why all the secrecy on the phone? What

did the report say? I stopped by the house on my way out of town, but I didn't have mine."

"Mine came this morning, Ross."

"And?" He could feel his heart rate accelerate.

She looked at him for a moment.

"Mel, please. Just tell me." His impatience came through in his tone.

She cleared her throat. "She isn't yours, Ross. You're not Keri's father." She looked somber; her voice sounded weak.

Ross was silent feeling at once relieved and disappointed.

"I found myself not wanting to open the letter when it arrived, and then, when I did read it, I couldn't help but feel disappointment." Her blue eyes had a far-away, sad look about them.

"I'll still be here for you, if you need me. And for Keri, if she needs me, Mel. I've told you that. The test results don't change that."

"I know you said that before." Her blue eyes focused on him once again. "You're too good, Ross. And, thank you. I mean that sincerely." She touched his arm gently.

"On the phone, you said you wanted to warn me about something," he prompted, looking down into her eyes.

"Yes, I do. And I'm afraid you're going to be angry with me. I hardly know where to begin."

"Just tell me, Mel. Don't play word games. Just say it."

She sighed. "The person I want to warn you about is Michael Kerns."

Ross's forehead creased in a frown. His suddenly cold eyes now bore into her. "How do you know Michael?" He demanded.

"Please, Ross, don't raise your voice. It's a long story. Michael and I go back a ways."

"I'm all ears," he said coolly. "Start at the beginning, take all the time you need." Ross crossed his arms tightly across his chest and leaned rigidly against the back of the stone bench.

She began speaking softly. "It started while you and I were still married."

"Not him, too!"

"No. As I was trying to tell you, I was seeing Richard. I told you I was visiting friends, but Richard and I were actually spending those weekends in Atlantic City. Richard loved the tables, and I played the machines. We did pretty well. Michael spent a lot of time there, too. Richard, being in pharmaceutical sales, knew Michael. He introduced us, and we partied together. There were others too. We used to plan our weekends so that we could all meet. That's where I met Kevin Williams."

"For God's sake, Melanie. Just what…"

"Please, Ross. I'm trying to explain. Kevin and Michael were great friends. We all had some pretty wild weekends back then. I found out that Lil was Kevin's aunt, but he swore me to secrecy. I was never quite sure why. I guess he just wanted to contact her in his own time." She was quiet for a moment.

"I have a feeling his time never would have come if Maggie hadn't shown up in Serenity. But, go on, Melanie. Tell me more."

She had been standing for the last few moments, now she sat down. He shifted on the bench to face her.

"Did Michael put you up to getting in touch with me? Was it his idea for you to say that you still cared for me? That you wanted us to try again? Tell me exactly how he figures in to all this?"

"Ross, please."

"Is that how you were planning to break Maggie and me up?" he cut in. His face flushed as he rose angrily from the bench and turned to face her. "You would condescend to come back into my life? I suppose you thought I wouldn't be able to resist you if you came back with a child. That I'd take you back with open arms, and that would free Maggie up for Michael to try to move back in on her. Then she could bail him out of the financial mess he'd got himself into. Is that pretty much the scenario, Melanie?"

"No. No. It isn't like that." Her eyes were tearing. "I mean that is what Michael wanted when he approached me, but that isn't how it was with me. "

"Give me a break, Melanie. I'm not stupid. Just because you lied to me in the past and I..."

"Listen to me," she cut in. "Please hear me out. I didn't have to tell you any of this, you know. I'm telling you because I *truly do care* about you. You've been terrific, and I *don't* want you to get hurt."

He was thoughtful for a moment. "Okay. I guess you're right. You didn't have to tell me." He sounded calmer. "Go on. I won't interrupt you." He sat down and leaned back against the bench once again.

"I hadn't seen Michael in months. He called me one night. I think it was in August, or maybe it was September. But that doesn't really matter anyway. He called, and he told me he was in deep trouble, and he just needed a friend to talk to. He wanted to borrow some money, but I told him I didn't have any to spare, that Richard was out of the picture. He said he needed to get this girl back, that she could help him out of this jam, and the girl turned out to be Maggie. He said she was in Serenity.

"After that, we talked often—several times a week. Then, all of a sudden, he said he'd just learned that Maggie and my ex were an item. Kevin had told him. He said Kevin was trying to work out an arrangement for him with the IRS. He said they had a scheme they thought might cause you two to break up, and Michael might have a chance of getting back with Maggie, since she was pregnant, and he thought it was his baby. Of course, that plan included me. He wanted me to tell you that Keri was yours. If Michael and Maggie got back together, he thought it would make a considerable dent in the money he owes, maybe wipe out his debt completely. At one point, Michael was scared to death that he might have to do some time for income tax evasion, but that seems to have been worked out."

"So, you agreed to help your old friend out?"

"No. I didn't to begin with. But, he kept after me. I even thought of having my number changed so he'd leave me alone. But then, he started sounding so desperate that I didn't want to make him angry. I was afraid of what he might do. And I couldn't afford to move.

"I just kept thinking about you. The more he talked about you and Maggie, the more I wanted to see you again, Ross. And, not to help Michael. Just simply and selfishly for me, because I found myself thinking about you almost constantly. I thought about how it was between us in the beginning, and I began feeling the fool for all I gave up." She paused for a minute and inhaled deeply. "The choices we make," she said softly. She looked off into the distance.

Ross shook his head slowly. "Melanie, Melanie."

"I know. It all sounds incredible. Small world and all those cliches, huh? Anyway, I could see after we met again that you had changed. That you didn't have feelings for me any longer, that you really do love Maggie. And in spite of everything past and present, you were trusting and supportive of me and so good with Keri. I just couldn't live with myself if I didn't level with you, if I didn't warn you about Michael."

Ross sat quietly shaking his head as if he were still trying to digest it all.

"I've talked to Kevin, and he's worried too," she continued. He's pretty much washed his hands of Michael."

Sure he has, Ross thought, t*o save his own butt.* He kept his thoughts to himself. Telling Melanie about his meeting with Kevin would serve no purpose. He became aware that Melanie was still talking.

"Kevin told him to leave you two alone, but I'm not sure Michael is listening to anyone. I'm not sure what all is troubling him. I think he may even be on drugs. He's very unstable these days. He has tremendous pressure on him. Just seems to be out of control. Kevin says he's been put on temporary leave at the hospital, and he was on probation before that. He needs a lot of help," Melanie said shaking her head. "The doctor in charge of the lab I work for said it sounded like borderline personality disorder to him. I didn't name Michael, but I told him a bit about his behavior. He had a lot of the symptoms of an identity disorder, too."

"What you've told me seems to explain the threatening phone call I had last night. I feel sure it was Michael"

"Oh, Ross, he frightens me. This gives me chills. What did he say?"

"Someone called and told me to call off the wedding. Said it would never take place. It was a man. It had to be Michael. I wouldn't be surprised if he wasn't having someone go through the mail at the house before I get home. That could explain why I haven't received my report like you did."

"It could be. He really needs professional help! You can see why I had to warn you. Why I wanted you and Maggie to be aware that you need to watch out for him. I'm not sure what he's capable of at this point."

"Thanks, Mel. Sorry I was so tough on you earlier. I do appreciate your honesty, and the warning. We'll be in touch. You know how to reach us if you need to."

"I hope Maggie realizes just how lucky she is."

"I'm the lucky one. She's wonderful, Mel."

"I've heard she is, Ross. I really do hope you have a long, happy life together. You deserve it."

They embraced briefly before Ross turned and walked to his car. If he had looked back, he'd have seen Melanie watching him with tears rolling down her cheeks. But, he didn't look back.

Chapter Twenty-Eight

The return trip to Serenity was uneventful. Ross reached the town limits within forty-five minutes. All the way back, he was unable to force his concerns about Michael from his mind. Just what *was* the man capable of? This was too risky for him to handle on his own. Once in town he drove directly to Sheriff George Barton's office. The men spent nearly an hour together before Ross left and went to Maggie's.

When she opened the door he gathered her into his arms and held her tightly to him. She pulled back a little and kissed him. "I think I'll have to send you up to see Melanie every once in a while, if this is the greeting I get when you come back to me," she said smiling at him.

"I've missed you today, Maggie," he said, still holding her. "Saturday can't come soon enough for me."

They went into the kitchen, and she began preparing dinner for them while he filled her in on the afternoon starting with his and Melanie's conversation, and concluding with the terrible accident that had delayed him on his way to meet her.

"Oh, Ross, when will this end?" She sounded weary.

"Soon, I hope. I stopped by Sheriff Barton's before I came here. He's going to keep an eye on you right up until the time you say 'I do.' He'll be there at the wedding with backup, and if Michael shows his face anywhere around that church, he'll have an official escort out of town."

Maggie took a deep breath and shook her head. She served one of Ross's favorites, pork-chops, stuffing, green beans and yeast rolls. "Would you like a glass of wine?"

"You wouldn't happen to have a cold beer, would you?"

"I think there might be one or two left from when we had pizza." She opened the refrigerator door and moved a couple of containers. "You're in luck, there are three bottles of Michelob here," she said, removing one and handing it to him.

"One will do," he told her twisting the cap off.

...

Thursday was busy for Maggie and the women. She spent most of the day with Caroline, Lil and Marion Townlee. Preparations were well under control. By Friday, Maggie was ready to concentrate on preparing for her aunts' arrival later that day. Lil had offered to let them sleep at her place since she had two guestrooms, but Maggie said they'd be just fine in her room if they didn't mind sharing a bed. She planned to take the couch.

Their plane was due in at two-twenty that afternoon. Ross reached the Raleigh-Durham airport vicinity with time to spare. He decided to stop at a little roadside café near the airport to buy a hot dog and a coke. When the cashier rang up his tab it came to $5.89.

"This hot dog had better be the best I've ever eaten," he told the elderly woman operating the cash register.

"It'll be one to remember anyway," she said with a wink. "I could almost guarantee that."

He took a bite as he left the café. It was tasty but, not $5.89 good. As he drove away, he couldn't help but wonder how long they'd be in business with prices like that, good or not.

...

The U.S. Air Express flight was right on time. Maggie had shown Ross a picture of her aunts, so he was watching for them as the passengers came up the departure ramp. They were the last two people off the plane. Both looked a bit bewildered as they walked, arms linked, into the gate 47 waiting area. There was no mistaking that the two were sisters, and they still looked just like their picture, though Maggie had told him it was a few years old. Tall and slender, both had gray blue eyes and the same short, tightly permed, gray hair with more than a little hint of blue in it. One wore a dark blue coat, the other was dressed in forest green.

Ross stepped over to the two elderly ladies. "Clara and Emily, I presume?"

"And you must be Ross. I'm Clara," the one in blue said. "And this is Emily."

Ross extended his hand to Clara first.

"Nonsense," Clara said, taking his hand and pulling him closer. She gave him a bear hug. "We're practically family. The Martin girls have always been huggers, and we're too old to change now."

Ross laughed, "I'm with you on that one." After embracing them both, he said, "Now, if you ladies will come with me and point out your luggage on the conveyer belt, we'll be on our way."

...

There was no lack of conversation during the drive back to Serenity. The sister's were excited about the plane ride. Clara had flown only twice before, and that had been when she was much younger. This was Emily's first flight. It was quite evident, after only a few moments that Clara was the more gregarious, a "mother hen" taking care of her older sister whose eyesight was beginning to fade. Both had lively personalities though and seemed genuinely thrilled to be a part of their favorite niece's wedding.

The conversation made the ride home seem much shorter than the trip up. As they drove into Serenity, Clara exclaimed, "Wow! Just look at that, Em. I'll bet this whole place looks just like a Thomas Kincaid painting in the springtime."

"Oh my yes. How utterly charming! I'll bet you're right, Clara," Emily chimed in.

Minutes later, they turned into the driveway and parked in front of Maggie's apartment. Before they were out of the car, Maggie bounded through the door at the foot of the stairs. There were hugs and kisses, and a few tears shed by all three.

Ross couldn't suppress a smile. "You girls go on up," he told them. "I'll bring the luggage."

Before they reached the top of the stairs, Maggie knew that Ross had won them over.

"He's absolutely wonderful, Maggie!" Clara raved, "And is he handsome? Oh my, yes!"

"Oh my, yes, is right," Emily agreed. "And such a good conversationalist. You know what I mean, dear. Lot's of men don't talk much. You're Uncle Wiley never did, God rest his soul," she added quickly. "And what a charming little village, Maggie. I can see why you didn't want to leave!"

When they reached the living room, Aunt Clara said, "Stand back young lady and let me have a look at you. I believe there's something you forgot to tell us."

Maggie laughed, "You're right. I did."

"Well," Aunt Clara said. "I have to admit I'd have had a hard time sayin no to that young man myself."

"Oh my, Clara. Shame on you!" Aunt Emily chided.

Ross stepped into the living room and carried their suitcases on into the bedroom. Maggie stuck her head into the room. "Guess you already know you've got them eating out of your hand. They think you're Mr. Wonderful."

He looked at her and smiled. "They're corkers, Maggie. We had a great time on the ride home." He kissed her before they went back into the living room to join Clara and Emily.

Lil, Caroline and Charlie joined them for a while, but they left by nine-thirty to be "rested for the big day." Ross left the three 'girls', as he referred to them, at eleven.

"I'm certainly glad this is the last night we'll have to part at bedtime," he whispered into her ear when she walked with him to the door.

The girls stayed up for another thirty minutes, reluctant to say goodnight after such a pleasant evening of reminiscences and catching-up.

Throughout the night, two unmarked cars patrolled the street outside Maggie's house.

Chapter Twenty-Nine

Saturday, Maggie and Ross's wedding day, dawned a perfect December morning in Serenity, North Carolina. The sun was bright; the high was expected to be around fifty. Maggie was the first one up at her apartment. She moved quietly into the kitchen and turned on the coffee maker. Within minutes, the smell of freshly brewing decaf drifted through the little apartment.

By the time Clara and Em joined Maggie in the kitchen, she had stirred up a batch of blueberry muffins, and they were rising in the oven.

"Oh, my dear, you shouldn't be waiting on us on your wedding day."

"I'm happy to do it, Aunt Clara," Maggie said, giving each aunt a little squeeze. "I'm so glad you're here with me for this day." She felt her eyes begin to tear.

Quickly, Maggie went to the oven and opened the door to check the muffins. "I think they're done," she said, when the toothpick she stuck into one came out clean. She set them on a baker's rack to cool.

"Now don't those look like the best muffins you've ever seen, Clara?" Emily asked. "And don't they smell just mouthwateringly delicious?"

"Oh my, yes. They do!" Clara agreed.

. . .

By half-past-twelve, Maggie had begun dressing for the most important day in her life. She took special care with her make-up, and after she brushed the earth tone, eye shadow onto her lids and brow, she dotted just a touch of aqua in the inner corners of her lids. Then, she smoothed it over the lid with her fingertips to bring out the color of her eyes. She brushed a bit of color onto her cheeks and applied her lipstick last.

She went to her closet and removed the ivory-colored two-piece silk wedding dress and laid it on her bed. She removed the clear plastic covering. She stepped into the ankle length skirt and pulled it up around her tummy. She straightened the side seams and smoothed the skirt down over her hips. She turned to make sure that the slit was in the exact center of the back, then she slid the over-blouse from the hanger and slipped it over her head. She looked at herself in the mirror. It fit her perfectly today, as she had allowed a little extra room when she purchased it two weeks ago. The pearl and iridescent beaded top shimmered softly under the indirect bedroom lighting. She had had a difficult time choosing between this outfit and another, but today she was so glad she had selected this one. It was very flattering in the way it minimized her ever expanding mid-section.

Now she was ready to style her hair. She put a clean white towel around her shoulders and began brushing her hair. Then she swept her chestnut locks up onto the top of her head and fastened a circular comb around it to hold it in place. She left a few wispy tendrils about her face. Ross always like her hair when she wore it up, and today this style would be perfect with the miniature white orchid and baby's breath floral headpiece she fastened into her upswept hair. She slipped her feet into a pair of cream-colored satin pumps and took one last look in the mirror.

She went into the living room to join her aunts who had finished dressing a short time earlier. As she entered the room, they drew in their breath in unison.

"Oh, my dear," Emily said. "You look exquisite!" She took a tissue from her pocket and wiped her eyes.

"Absolutely lovely! Wouldn't our Lucy have been proud? Your father and Jill would've been too," Clara said, her voice breaking as she spoke. She, too, dabbed at her eyes. "I'm afraid that even with the sun shining, it's going to be a wet afternoon." She managed a chuckle before blowing her nose.

Maggie glanced at the clock on her kitchen wall. "I guess it's time. I'll call Charlie and Caroline and let them know we're ready."

...

Caroline's eyes teared the minute she saw Maggie. She hugged Maggie to her and sobbed softly.

Maggie knew exactly what was going through her mind, and her heart ached for Caroline. "I'm so glad you and Charlie are in my life," she whispered into her ear. "And that you're a part of this special day."

Caroline released Maggie and nodded. "Me, too, dear," she managed to whisper back.

Charlie walked over to the garage to back the car out. Maggie noticed that he stopped to wipe his eyes and blow his nose before getting into the vehicle.

...

When they arrived at the church, Maggie noticed that Ross's car was already there. So far, it was devoid of decoration. She was grateful. It would attract no undue attention that way.

Maggie and Charlie went in through the side door that opened into a small room near the altar. Ross had been instructed to go to the room on the opposite side of the altar. Caroline and the aunts walked around to the front of the church.

Reverend Townlee was in the room waiting for Maggie and Charlie, as the two stepped inside.

"Maggie Thornton, we may have to change the order of this occasion slightly, but don't let anything that happens this afternoon trouble you. Just follow Doc's lead. Okay?" He didn't wait for her answer. "Now, would you come with me for a minute, Charlie?"

Maggie looked at him in surprise. The two men turned and left the room. "Now what did he mean by that?" she asked aloud of no one.

A few moments later, Charlie rejoined her. "Alright little girl, they're ready for us to go around to the front of the church."

"Did you see Ross when you left?"

"I did. He's waiting for you." Charlie put his hands on Maggie's shoulders and looked down into her eyes. "Before we go back there, I just want to tell you how proud we are of you and how much you mean to Caroline and me. I know you haven't been part of our lives for very long, but it feels like you have."

"You know how special you both are to me." She kissed his cheek. She noticed that his face flushed a bit.

Charlie cleared his throat. "We'd better get back there now. Wouldn't do for them to start without us, would it?"

...

Just after Maggie and Charlie stepped inside the church, and the doors closed behind them, a black Mercedes drove down the street. It pulled into the church parking lot. Two other cars, both white Fords, pulled onto the side street and parked.

...

Lil and Bobby Hensley were waiting for Maggie and Charlie in the narthex of the church. Lil grinned her broadest when she saw Maggie, and Bobby ran to her and threw his arms around her waist.

"Wow, Maggie! You're the beautifulist bride I've ever seen," his brown eyes danced with excitement.

"And just how many brides have you seen, Bobby?" Lil wanted to know. "But you're right, honey. She's about the beautifulist I've seen, too."

Maggie laughed. "We're all beautiful, Bobby. You look so handsome today, like a real little man in your cutaway. She thought Lil looked the perfect matron-of-honor with her smiling blue eyes and wearing a lovely silver-gray crepe dress with matching shoes and gloves. She'd made a special trip to Raleigh to find "just the right dress" for the occasion.

Charlie and Maggie stood arm in arm, awaiting Marion's cue for Ross to step to the front of the altar so that Maggie and Charlie could start down the aisle. At last the note sounded!

Ross stepped out of the door to the left of the altar, followed by Doc Miller. They stood before Reverend Townlee and turned to watch Maggie begin her walk toward Ross and their future together. The expression on Ross's face as he glimpsed his bride left no doubt in anyone's mind as to how he felt about Maggie. It brought a tear to Maggie's eyes, as she smiled back at this man, who, in a matter of months, had come to mean the world to her. Who could have dreamed that day in August, as she left Alexandria in despair, that she would find such joy a few months later with a wonderful man in a tiny town called Serenity?

Heads turned as Maggie and Charlie proceeded down the aisle. When Maggie was only a few steps from Ross, she saw Doc's expression change. He nodded toward someone behind her, then he whispered something to Ross.

Ross reached out and took Maggie's arm. With his other hand he grabbed Bobby's wrist. He pulled them forward and hurried them into the small room at the side of the altar where Maggie had been when she first arrived at the church.

Charlie stopped and stood at the entrance to the front pew where Caroline, and Kathryn Miller were seated. Kathryn rose and quickly stepped into the center aisle. She moved to the front of the church and took her place beside her husband.

"Friends," Reverend Townlee addressed the congregation. "We are gathered here today to celebrate the renewal of vows of our dear friends Kathryn and Andrew Miller, better known to all of you as Doc."

From behind the closed door, Maggie asked, "What's going on, Ross?"

"Yeah," Bobby added. "I need to know too!"

"Shhhh!" Ross said, gently cupping his hand over Bobby's mouth. Just trust me, both of you. This will all be over soon."

Maggie moved closer to the door and peered out of the small window at the top of the door.

There was a loud commotion at the back of the church. Suddenly, a man burst through the back doors of the sanctuary and started down the aisle. He reached into his coat pocket and removed a black metal object. A shot rang out; the bullet lodged in the rafters overhead. Two men at the back of the congregation jumped up and ran toward him. Two deputies entered behind him, with weapons drawn.

"Hold it right there! Stop! Put the gun down, and get your hands in the air or I *will* shoot!" Sheriff Barton's booming bass voice was commanding.

Bobby fell to the floor. Ross leaned down and whispered to him. "Just stay real quiet, Bobby. Everything's gonna be fine." Ross lifted the boy up into his arms patting his back gently to calm him.

Beyond the door in the sanctuary, Maggie could see that the intruder had stopped. There was a wild look in his green eyes as the tall, dark-haired man turned to face the sheriff. Still holding the gun, he stretched his arms above his head. His motions were jerky, he appeared dazed, confused.

"Where's the wedding party?" he demanded. "Where's Maggie Thornton? I'm not going to hurt anyone. I just want Maggie!" he demanded angrily, looking around the church.

Maggie turned back to Ross. "I need to go out there before some innocent people get hurt," she whispered. "Maybe I can talk some sense into him. It's me he wants." Her hand shook as she reached for the doorknob.

'Absolutely not!" Ross was adamant. "Let them handle it. It's their job."

Bobby reached out and grabbed Maggie's shoulder. "No. No. Don't go!" His little face clouded up, and tears began rolling down his cheeks.

They heard Sheriff Barton's voice again, "Okay, mister, just hold real still. We don't need any accidents today. Just drop that gun nice and slow now, and everything's gonna be fine. And nobody's gonna get hurt."

There wasn't a sound to be heard in the church. The man looked about, arms still in the air, and realizing himself surrounded by four armed men, slowly opened his hand and let the weapon fall to the floor. Sheriff Barton pulled the intruder's arms down behind his back and secured the handcuffs about his wrists. His deputy grabbed one of the man's arms; the sheriff held the other.

"Where's the wedding party?" the man asked again, in a loud voice. "Where's Maggie? Just tell me that!"

"Here's the wedding party, young man," Doc said

calmly. "My wife and I are renewing our vows today, and I don't believe you were on our guest list."

The interloper still looked stunned as he was escorted out of the church and taken to a patrol car.

...

Ross gently lowered Bobby onto the floor. He and Maggie breathed a sigh of relief. "Now, Bobby," Maggie said leaning down to the child. "Let's dry those tears before we go out there."

Bobby ran the backs of his hands under his eyes. "Those aren't tears, Maggie. My eyes just leak sometimes. I wasn't scared!"

Maggie shook her head and grinned at Ross.

There was a knock at the door. "Let's get on with this happy occasion," Reverend Townlee said, as the door swung open. Maggie and Ross stepped up to the altar for the second time on their wedding day.

...

As they started down the aisle toward the back of the church, Maggie whispered into her new husband's ear. "Can't we do anything in a normal way? Do you suppose this is how it will go for the rest of our lives? At least no one will ever call us boring."

"I expected your first words as my wife might be something far more romantic, Mrs. Harrington. Like, I can't wait to get you alone or I want your body desperately," he whispered back and kissed her cheek.

"That's a given, Mr. Harrington." She looked up at her husband and winked.

...

The wedding party and all of the guests moved to the basement of the library. It had been chosen to host the reception, as it would accommodate more people than the fellowship hall. The room was abuzz with talk of the wedding. Everyone was in agreement that this had been the most unusual wedding ever in Serenity, probably one of the most unique anywhere. And, by far, the most exciting!

The guests had been alerted as they arrived to the possibility of a "little interruption" but no one, except for Matt Hensley, was given any clue as to what they might expect. They certainly didn't want to take the chance of him having a relapse so soon after his heart attack. He had insisted he'd be fine and wouldn't hear of staying home. He'd said he'd be much more anxious not being there, as his imagination might work overtime. Everyone else had been instructed to remain calm and in their seat and not to show surprise at anything. They were also assured that the matter was under control. Everyone had handled the situation beautifully.

"I'm sorry we had to let things get so far," Jeff Farnsworth, one of the deputies who had returned for the reception, told the newlyweds. "But we had to give him enough time to make his move, so we'd have legal grounds to arrest and hold him."

Clara and Emily couldn't stop talking about it. "I'm certainly glad you broke it off with *that Michael*," Clara told Maggie animatedly. "Even if he is a doctor, he turned out to be a real honest to goodness *nut*! He needs to treat himself, wouldn't you say?"

"Oh my, yes!" Emily agreed wholeheartedly. "I was just wondering, Clara. Do you think this qualifies as a shotgun wedding?" She chuckled at her own little joke.

Clara burst out laughing. "I'd say it does! Good one, Em. First literal shotgun wedding I've ever been to."

Ross chuckled and shook his head. "Corkers," he whispered in Maggie's ear.

Clara and Emily had gotten on quite well with Maggie's

friends. It had been arranged that Charlie and Caroline would take them to the airport the following day. They would spend tonight at Maggie's apartment.

So far, no one knew where the newlyweds would honeymoon, including Maggie. When Maggie and Ross were ready to leave the festivities, Ross tapped a spoon on his champagne glass. It took a few seconds for the room to become hushed.

"Before my wife and I leave you today, Maggie has an announcement she'd like to make."

All eyes focused on Maggie Harrington. She stood in front of what was left of the wedding cake Caroline had baked and decorated for them.

"I'd like to ask Diane Summers to step up here with us." She waited as Diane left Ryan's side and joined them. Then she continued.

"All of you have given me such a wonderful gift since that very first day I came to Serenity, and you've made me feel so welcome. You've given me your acceptance and friendship, and I treasure each of you. I've wanted to give something back to all of you. Ross and I have decided on a way to do it.

"We've arranged to have an addition built onto the library. It will allow the children's section to add a third more books than it currently houses, and the same will be added in the general section."

She turned to Caroline and Charlie before continuing. "The addition will be known as the Joy Keller Memorial Wing. Construction is set to begin in about a month. Diane has a blueprint and mock-up of the project upstairs. You're all welcome to stop in. She'll be happy to share it with you."

Caroline and Charlie approached Maggie and Ross. "I don't know how to thank you," Caroline whispered through her tears.

"You already have." Maggie embraced them both.

...

When they were finally alone in Ross's car, he asked, "Where would you like to spend your honeymoon, Mrs. Harrington? I decided to let you name the place. Anywhere! The Bahamas? Paris? Rome? Just tell me your hearts desire, and I'll take you there."

Maggie hesitated only a moment before replying. "Take me to paradise, Ross. That's where I want to spend our honeymoon."

"And where might this paradise be?"

"It won't take long to get there, and when we do, we'll find a lovely old home with green shutters and a porch that spans three quarters of the house. And there's a beautiful little pond we can fish in and a bridge where we can watch the sun rise and set. The most remarkable man I've ever known has been tending to it lovingly for a very long time. And now, all I want is to spend the rest of my life there, loving him and loving it the way he does."

Ross turned into the gravel lane that led to their home and stopped the car. He turned off the ignition and took Maggie in his arms. "I love you, Maggie Thornton Harrington. I'll love you forever and beyond."

He slowly removed the wedding band from her finger and held it up so she could read the engraving. "Forever and Beyond."

He slipped it back onto her ring finger and wrapped his hand firmly around hers.

"Forever and beyond," she whispered against her husband's lips.